# Fairytales for Femmes

*Seven magic bedtime stories about*

*the power of love ...*

# Fairytales

## For

## L. Holm

**Solibris
Publishers**

Original edition 2009

Copyright © 2009 L.Holm

Illustrations © L.Holm

Published by Solibris Publishers; Lund, Sweden
www.solibris-publishers.com

ISBN 978-91-978383-0-6
Printed in the United States of America.

"How
do you define a person?
The only person that ever was?
For you?
Always?

How
do you speak to her?
After an eternity of hope
without hope?

How do you look at her
without falling apart
inside?"

# Contents

1. The Love of My Life — 1
2. The Event — 25
3. Pink Magic — 47
4. The Beholder — 65
5. One Way Ticket to Always — 89
6. Date night, right? — 107
7. Harmony of the Spheres — 129

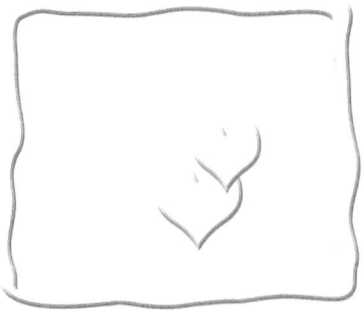

## "The Love of My Life"

W hy did this woman have to live at the end of nowhere?

I had been driving for more than three hours and I was getting fed up. The radio station played old tunes from the '80s and I sang along, bumping up and down in my '69 Mercury Cougar Eliminator, focusing on the highs and lows of the crooked dirt path in front of me. The sound of my own voice started to get on my nerves.

But if I didn't sing I would start to think, and that was never a good idea.

Surrounded by the breath of thousands of trees, I was reminded of all the anonymous deaths that were taking place in secret places everywhere.

When I was a little girl, the forest was my sanctuary, my only place of shelter and refuge. I had loved the creatures that lived there and the big trees that used to talk to me when I was lost; all those lonely nights when faraway stars twinkled like Christmas decorations in my frightened face.

Light long overdue, lingering in the black sky, watching over me, reflecting my inner void with its own eternal bliss. When you are a star, death is just an illusion. Twinkle, twinkle little star, still going strong. Pretending that you are.

As I grew older I turned to my own species for comfort. One misplaced obsession after the other made me realize how different I was in the only way that really matters. But by then the old trees had stopped talking to me, leaving me bereft of hope, alone and strange in a hostile world.

Money came to me when I was still young; from dead people I had hated and feared when they were alive. The cold sheen of their memory hovered over me like a legacy of cruelty, since the combination of too much money and no pride whatsoever made me incredibly attractive in the eyes of others.

Once independently wealthy, I suddenly found myself surrounded by women who could smell the molecules of my crisp money from miles away. They followed in my trail like persistent vampires disguised as butterflies and for the first time in my life I enjoyed the game of being pursued, hunted down and taken advantage of.

Somewhere along my destructive path an expert of the human mind took me under her maternal wing and I told myself that I loved her. Or maybe she told me, and I believe her? After all, it was her calling to deconstruct people and restore them to her own liking, and her reputation was spotless.

After three years of intensive therapy, day and night, I realized that thanks to her, my mistress of madness, I had ended up more mentally and sexually screwed up than ever.

By then my libido was my only vital trait, my only means of connection, so I cherished, nurtured, worshipped it obsessively, compulsory, feverishly, because I secretly, silently prayed that someday, somewhere, the big black O of oblivion, the ultimate Orgasm, would take mercy on me and claim me back to the Void; the home of all dead light.

Now I was on my way to meet a kindred spirit in the gigantic global club of Self-Haters Anonymous. I had purchased a ridiculously expensive bottle of Château d´Yquem and a bottle of Springbank single malt whisky for my date, just for the fun of it.

Just for the pleasure of watching her expression and make an evaluation of her greed, acting skills or ignorance, at a vantage point.

My date "Gina", officially known as Lady-GEE on the net, was famous for being very good at all the nice things you can imagine, and excellent at things so bad you can't even begin to imagine them until you've tried them. But by then, of course, nice is no longer an option. But I didn't need any options. All I needed was a quick fix of the cruelest drug on earth: anonymous sex, the drug of temporary annihilation; the drug of my choice. Too much money and too much self-hatred is a bad combination. Whatever you do to ease your pain you end up hating yourself even more, because you pay a fortune for people to abuse you, the way they would happily abuse any dirt poor bastard for free just for the fun of it.

I steered my impressive engine up a small hill and there it was, just like "Gina" had described it in her emails; a small cabin surrounded by lots of old, kind oak trees. I didn't dare to think what that perverted woman might do to those beautiful trees.

Small lights lit up the small windows like fake stars. Now those small beacons of hope were guiding me to the little death at the end of my road.

I parked my Mercury Eliminator on the lawn in front of her house.

My black leather trousers adorned with leather suspenders caressed my shapely legs and delicious ass, while the black leather bra under the see-through lace vest fondled my breasts. An oversized black and white striped Armani jacket hung loosely over my shoulders to add just a touch of class. I looked great from any angle and in any position imaginable and I knew it. I planted my Doc Martens boots firmly on the ground, placed an irresistible smile on my face, and pushed the bell.

When she opened the door I was taken aback for a second.

She didn't look at all what I had expected from her description. She wore plain clothes: a grey t-shirt, baggy army surplus trousers, and flat leather sandals on her feet. Her long chestnut hair fell in wild and unruly locks down her back. Her eyes were big and blue like a summer's day in a children's book. The gaze in those beautiful eyes made me think of a very young person, or someone too fragile for the hassles of life.

"Hello!" she said.

Her voice was shy but warm and I could tell she was extremely nervous. Well, maybe that was a good sign. After all, I hadn't come all this way to play a game of Scrabble.

"Gee!" I said with my sexiest, huskiest voice, flashing the darkness of my soul into the depths of her soul, and stepped inside.

Her mind processed my bold words and manners for a few seconds, like they were a strange language she had once mastered. Then she suppressed a smile that migrated to her blue eyes.

"You look surprised?" I said and tilted my head in a cocky manner I knew most women not yet dead found irresistible. "Why? Not what you expected?"

"No...!"

She blushed. And smiled. It was a smile devoid of cynicism. Or lust for that matter.

"Sorry! I didn't mean to be rude!" she said. "I don't own a wristwatch. But you are a bit early..."

She paused.

"Aren't you?"

"Not that early, I hope?" I said flirtatiously.

She blushed again. Made a gesture to the stains on her grey Ramones t-shirt and baggy trousers.

"No! Of course not! But look at me! I haven't changed clothes, or anything!"

She cleared her throat and said:

"Welcome! I have really been looking forward to this. I really hope I won't make you disappointed!"

"Let's say I am prepared to give you a fair chance."

She gave me a warm smile.

"Thank you! And thank you for being so understanding. Well, I guess I just forgot about time."

We shook hands. Nice beginning, but not a major turn-on in the foreplay department.

Her hand was surprisingly strong and left a small spot of red oil paint on my own right hand.

I wondered about the significance of this for a second. *"Red? Stain? Hand?"*
The semantic implications escaped me. Maybe I should have studied the fine prints of her emails more carefully.

I gave her the plastic bag, and she let out a small sigh when she peeked into the bag and saw the two bottles.

"Wow! But this is ...! You are too generous!"

"I hope not!"

She smiled, and sighed, as if relieved.

Then she leaned forward and hugged me. It was a sweet hug, a teddy bear hug, and not one bit sexy or seducing. I could feel her soft breast under the thin t-shirt against my leather bra and the hard bottles against my back. She smelt good. Not a hint of perfume, just a tiny bit of sweat, turpentine, soap and coffee in a pleasant mix.

But she had forgotten to mention how thin she was. How fragile she would feel in my arms.

The small house welcomed me into its warm and cozy heart. A nice smell of artist's fumes lingered in the air and mixed with the fragrance of coffee and the scent from a wooden bowl of potpourri.

A handmade bright red rag-rug covered the grey hardwood tiles.

The room was furnished with a tasteful mix of old and new furniture, probably mostly inherited things, and some new items from IKEA. The walls were painted in earthy plum colors. In the middle of the floor stood an easel with a white canvas scarred with a few charcoal outlines.

The big oak dining-room table was overflowing with multitude of small glass bottles with different concoctions, mixtures, and solutions, and tubes with oil paint, tainted rags, and at least twenty different paintbrushes in different sizes. It reminded me of a miniature rain forest. A sanctuary for lost dreams.

The walls were decorated with unframed oil paintings of naked women. At a closer look, I could tell they were all portraits of the same extraordinarily beautiful woman with long blonde hair and penetrating cold eyes. She looked cruel and dominant. I liked her immediately. Maybe she would join us later? For dessert?

"Nice!" I said and nodded to the paintings.

She closed her eyes and formed her lips to a "yes" directed to herself or some spirit present in the room.

A moment later, when she handed me my glass of wine, her hand was trembling.

"Was this a bad idea? Please tell me, I really don´t mind. I want to know …what you think… about me… about this …I mean … I was so nervous …about you coming all the way … just to … just to…to… it's a strange situation …"

For someone so shy she was incredibly talkative. The sweet sounds that came from her mouth hypnotized me. I couldn't keep my eyes off her beautiful blue eyes that sparkled with light when she spoke, or her hands that moved like small birds in the air, or that beautiful sensual mouth of hers begging to be silenced by a kiss.

Suddenly her voice got serious, and I started to pay attention to what she was saying:

"...so hard to say goodbye to them when I love them so much."

"You ... *love* them? *All* of them?"

I couldn't believe my ears.

"But of course I love them all! They are my babies!"

"Well, you are quite a babe yourself! If I may say so!" I grinned.

She laughed.

"Will you love me too?" I asked, making silly sounds, with my hands close to my face trying to look and sound like an adorable puppy. Which I obviously didn't, despite my pleading eyes, because she laughed so hard she spilled fifty dollars worth of wine on the bright red rag rug.

"You have this weird sense of humor!" she said and made a jerking movement with her hand that caused her to spill another fifty dollars worth of wine, now on the grey hardboard floor. She smiled:

"Somehow I get this feeling you say one thing and mean something completely different!"

"Will you?" I insisted.

"But then I would have to paint you first! There are no shortcuts!"

"Clothes off, it is, then!" I teased.

She turned around so I couldn't watch her expression. I think she was embarrassed but she couldn't refrain from laughing.

"Tell me; which one's your favorite?" I asked.

"It's not here. It's in my bedroom."

"I figured."

She blushed.

All this blushing affected me in a strange way. You can't fake blushing can you? Fake an orgasm, yes! Easiest thing in the world! I picked up those skills very early in life. And fake dying? Yes! Definitely! It had come in handy a couple of times in my youth. But I couldn't blush if you held a gun to my head. (And this I knew for sure).

And all this blushing was because of me. She was so sweet I couldn't take my eyes of her. While she, on her part, was so nervous she couldn't return my glance for more than a few seconds, and then she would blush again.

Maybe I was not in such a hurry, after all. It was a long drive back on lonely roads. My libido could do with a little rest once in a while. I liked the way she looked and talked and smiled. I liked the way she accidentally kicked things over when she got excited, and for some reason I was intrigued by the way she sprinkled my vintage wine all over her place.

Soon I would leave all of this behind but I the mean time I might as well enjoy her with her clothes on; the way she moved her hands and interrupted her own speech with a big laugh; the way she blushed at her own jokes and tried to hide behind her wild mane of auburn hair.

She was absolutely adorable. The cutest thing I had ever seen.

I felt a strange feeling in my heart, the kind of tenderness I usually felt further down in my body on these occasions.

There might be a second date. For once I might make an exception to my rigid rules.

"Sorry I'm such a bad hostess; what will you think of me?"

"Well, to tell you the truth, you are not at all what I had expected." I said.

"Oh, no!"

Suddenly the bright light in her eyes died and I looked into the eyes of a forlorn woman. The sadness in those beautiful eyes almost knocked me to my feet. I wanted to drown in her big blue eyes. Rest in them forever. Make them look at me with love. I must be really tired.

"But you like my paintings? Don't you?" she said pleadingly. "You did say "*nice*"! Remember?"

She shrugged and straightening her back.

"Art for art's sake, then!" she said, sounding like a girl scout, all of a sudden.

Either she suffered from some multiple personality disorder, or she was really, really good at this game. But things weren't moving in the direction I wanted and had come all this way for, so I said:

"Do you get turned on when you do these kinds of things?"

She laughed.

"Of course not! Never! It's art! The human body is an exquisite piece of art. A reclining woman is beautiful. Not sexy. Don't you know that art is nature seen through a temperament?"

"Oh!" I said. "Maybe you are too disciplined when it comes to ... art? Perhaps you would enjoy your human nature even more if you allowed yourself some temper?"

Her sweet laugh had the effect of sparkling Champagne on me:

"You are so much fun, but why do I get the feeling it makes you makes you disappointed?"

I exposed my sharp white teeth in a big bad predatory grin:

"Honestly? You are telling me that when a gorgeous woman is posing naked in front of you, you feel nothing? Not even a little tingle in the juicy fruit?"

She looked appalled at my choice of words, so I quickly continued:

"Don't blame me if your paintings turn me on, with or without that artist-lingo temperament!"

She made some strange sounds and turned dark red. Her hands trembled so much she had to press the glass to her breast. She sounded like she was suffocating:

"You are ... very ... confident in your ... opinions. So ... direct... But of course I am glad I make you feel ... that way...about ...my paintings, I mean."

She cleared her throat, straightened her back and said in a neutral tone, trying to avoid making eye contact:

"Speaking as a connoisseur, you would make a wonderful model, you know."

She gave me a shy smile and continued:

"You have such a beautiful body! So strong and lean, ... and your energy is like that of a mountain lion ...so restless, ruthless, hungry ...almost like you are sniffing out a ... prey..."

She cleared her throat:

"I'm sure a painting of you in the nude would turn a lot of women on. Make them go berserk."

The compliment itself was okay, as compliments go, but she was too embarrassed to carry the tune. She buried her face in her hands and moaned:

"Oh no, I'm so bad at this...no wonder-..."

"No wonder... what?"

"I never- ..."

She was so nervous, I couldn't believe it. She couldn't make eye contact. The more I tried the less I could make her out.

She cleared her throat:

"Would you care for another glass of wine?" she said, suddenly the grand hostess again.

"Yes Ma'am!"

"And then I can show you my favorite painting in my bedroom? I call it "*The love of my life*".

"If your technique is only half as good as I suspect, it might get dangerous!"

She gave a start and stared at me, and there was a frightened note in her voice when she asked:

"What ... exactly do you mean?"

I smiled my most trustworthy smile.

"I'm only kidding, baby; please forgive me! I'm awful, awful!"

I touched her lightly on her arm and she closed her eyes. Then she looked at my hand as if she wanted to kiss it.

"No, I don't think you are awful."

I could tell her that she didn't. Her eyes were dark with emotion.

●

The bedroom was small and tidy. A beautiful grandmother's flowerbed quilt adorned the bed. Fresh plants thrived in the windowsills. An enormous bookcase covered one of the walls and it was filled with books. At a quick glance I could tell they were mostly romances, and books about art.

There was a huge painting of a naked woman watching us from above the pine commode. The cruel blonde, of course, more beautiful than ever, observing us from her elevated position.

"Do you do this a lot?" I said.

"O, no! My social skills are deteriorating. I have become a liability these days. I'm too impatient to participate in small talk and gossip and I always tend to say the wrong things, and laugh at the wrong places, and turn things over. Spill my wine, over people's best clothes, sofas. You know, after she died ... "

She was silent for a while. Then she said:

"I never leave this house. It was kind of you to drive all the way here."

"Well I don't know if *kind* is the word I would use."

She was breathing very hard.

She was either extremely nervous or very excited.

She avoided looking me in the eye and tried not to stand too close.

●

Apparently she needed lots of attention to get in the mood for sex and take her clothes off. But I didn't mind. I enjoyed this game.

"You are not what I expected." I said once again.

There was a strange tenderness in my voice I had never heard before. It surprised me more that it did her.

"You are disappointed with me, aren't you? I'm too introverted. Too Charlie Chaplin around people."

"I thought most painters were introverted? And he was definitely an extrovert."

"Well if you can imagine an introverted female Charlie Chaplin acting like an extroverted Charlie Chaplin around people, waving a paintbrush in the air with her sticky fingers, tripping people?"

The image made me laugh because I could easily imagine her at a party and I would have loved to be around to see her trip some of my avaricious acquaintances. She joined me laughing. Then she pointed at the woman over the commode.

"That's what she always used to say; you are such a fucking introvert! Not a nice thing to say, to someone you're supposed to love, is it?"

I changed the subject and moved closer to her to observe her blue eyes.

"From where do you get your inspiration?"

"From her."

I felt a stab of pure jealousy and touched her lightly on the shoulders.

"Wasn't she a lucky girl?"

＊

I touched her hair and kissed her on the throat. She closed her eyes and made some sounds that reminded me of a pleased cat.

"This is so new to me." She said. "I'm not ... used to... *this* ...anymore."

"I can tell." I said. "But you know what? It turns me on."

She gasped:

"I thought you said my paintings turned you on."

"Everything about you turns me on!" I said. "Except that ugly t-shirt of yours. I hate that group. Dysfunctional pricks!"

"Well I'm sorry. Because I happen to like them!"

"Don't be sorry! Just take it off. We'll see what happens?"

"You are very straight forward!"

"I am many things. Straight is not one of them. So please take it off."

"I didn't intend to... you mustn't believe ..."

"Believe what, baby?"

"That I set this up to seduce you."

"Let's just say I have never, ever met anyone as talented as you!"

She put her hands on my shoulders and pushed me away lightly, just to say:

"Please! I love too much. That's why I avoid situations like this. They always leave me, always, all of them, always, and then I'll ... die a little. And then I'll go and make another portrait of her. Better than the one before. Strange, isn't it?"

I started to hate the bitch over the commode. Any more lifelike and she might jump straight out of the painting and kick me in the groin, walking away with her finger in the air.

"You are so good at this!" I said. "So good it's ...insane, almost. And by the way, that lady over there belongs in a museum next to Mona Lisa. But Mona Lisa might not like the competition."

"Well, thank you! Yes, I do believe I have some talent!"

"Some? You do like to play wicked, wicked games with people's minds, don't you?"

She frowned and tried to protest but I put my index finger on her soft lips, playfully silencing her.

"And you like it rough." I said, adding a little pressure on my finger. "Don't you, baby? No mercy?"

I forced her to look into my eyes. Her eyes were dark with emotions now. I could feel her hot, unsteady breath on my lips. I removed my index finger from her moist lips and touched it with the tip of my own tongue, forcing her to meet my glance.

"...yes...no ... but..." she started, pale, and trembling like she was going to faint.

"But?"

"... I can't ... talk about it..."

I wouldn't dream of prolonging her torture so I silenced her with my kiss, letting my tongue explore the wet hot territory behind her lovely lips. I could tell she was starved for this game and after the initial chock of my forced entry, she groaned and thrust her arms around my neck, pressed her hips to mine, and hung onto my lips like I had just saved her from drowning. Or extinction.

"So is this standard procedure?" she asked a few minutes later, when we were trying to catch our breaths again.

"Gee, what do you want me to say? That I'm a borne again virgin?"

This made her laugh so hard she had to sit down on the bed.

"Oh no. No, no, no please don't tell me you are a virgin!"

She fell back on the bed laughing and I joined her. When the laughter subsided a different kind of energy grew on us. I let my hand slip under her t-shirt to caress her soft breast and play with her nipple.

At the sound of her pleasure I felt a stab of excitement between my legs that was so intense it was painful.

"I think you are wonderful." She whispered. "Gorgeous. Absolutely gorgeous."

I leaned over and kissed her, greedily, while teasing her erected nipple with my thumb and index finger. I forced her thighs apart with my leg. A tremor went through her body when my hip rubbed against her sex and she locked her thighs in a steel grip around my upper leg.

I tried not to give in to the overwhelming feeling of tenderness mixed with raw lust that was building up in me.

"I ... missed this ... so much." She whispered.

She pressed herself close to me. Buried her face between my breasts. Her words came in little gusts like she was out of breath.

"It has been so long ...I'm so ... excited ... hope I don't scare you!"

"Trust me, you don't scare me! But I love the way you try! I love your games. All of them!"

The touch of her strong hands when they slipped under my black leather bra and released my aching breasts was more than I could stand.

"I have to make love to you, baby..." I groaned.

By now I was so turned on I could hardly talk. Even my vision was blurred from the heat of my blood.

"Fuck me first! Make love to me later." She whispered.

That was our last exchange of comprehensible words. There was no need for words. I knew exactly what she wanted and where she would take us both. She had been very explicit on the net.

But she had forgotten to mention what her games would do to my heart.

●

Afterwards when I held her trembling body in my arms and buried my nose in her damp hair, she cried like a little girl.

"How did you know? I have never ever told anyone...

"I think we know each other quite well by now, don´t you?"

"Yes. Yes. Yes. We do." She said and for every "yes" she gave my hand a kiss. "And I love you."

"I love you, too." I whispered and kissed her neck. "I have never felt this way before."

"I fell in love with you the moment I saw you." She said. "I've never believed in love at first sight. Until today."

"Neither did I. Not until today."

She turned around in my arms and we kissed, softly, tenderly, deliciously this time.

"I didn't know what to do. I was so nervous!" She whispered.

I smiled and covered her face with tiny kisses.

I could smell me on her skin while I had the taste of her in my mouth.

"It seemed like the oldest trick in the book, seducing you just to make you exhibit my paintings."

"I have no intention of exhibiting your paintings, babe." I said.

"Why do you say that?"

I could feel her stiffen in my arms.

"Come on sweetie, you know that!" I said.

"So why did you come here? To seduce me?"

Panic was building up in her voice.

"Yes! Of course! I came for this!"

"For ... sex! You came to ... fuck me?"

There was pure horror in her eyes. She looked like had just woken up from a nightmare and was slowly realizing that every single detail of the nightmare was true. All the blood had vanished from her face.

"You used me!" she moaned.

The truth exploded in my face when I realized what she was saying. I jumped up from the bed and roared:

"God! I'm so fucking stupid! All the messages ... all the information ... just because you wanted someone loaded to exhibit your paintings."

She sobbed:

"You used me! You took advantage of my situation ...you knew about me!"

Her voice was filled with terror and her whole body was trembling now. She sounded like she was having an asthma attack.

"Of course I knew about you! Your advertising is all over the net!"

I grabbed my clothes and stumbled out of the house.

●

Never in my entire life had I felt so humiliated. Not even at gunpoint. Not even the first time. She had used me. Like the rest of them. She had been playing her game all along. Promoting her art. Art for art's sake.

On my way out of her house I grabbed the bottle of whisky and poured the burning liquor down my throat. I could hear her cry in the bedroom.

I staggered out on the lawn and collapsed.

Then I started to cry. For the first time in fifteen years I cried, and it was like all the pain and sadness I had stored inside emerged at the same time, determined to finish me off, once and for all.

I couldn't stop crying. I couldn't move. I was finally dying. This was what I had been praying for all these years.

The oak trees were whispering to me: *"The time has come baby girl, the time has come ..."*

But why did dying have to hurt so much? I wasn't prepared for the pain. I didn't deserve this much pain. I couldn't handle this much pain.

●

A red shining Mercedes-Benz cabriolet parked next to my filthy Eliminator and an elegant woman in high heels and an expensive haircut approached me, wrapped in a cloud of expensive perfume and an exquisite cashmere shawl, dressed in a formal grey business suit.

"And who the fuck are you?" I spat.

Snot was running down my nose, dripping on the ground, like slime from a wasted egg, slime from a wasted life; slime from slime, and dust to dust...

"My name is Catherine Colbert, the owner of Colbert & Colbin Art Gallery, downtown. I believe we spoke on the phone."

"No, I don't fucking believe we did."

"Sorry, I thought you must be Andrea! My mistake!"

"Andrea? You mean Gina?"

I spat out her name like a deadly curse. The effort made me wince.

"No, of course not! I mean Andrea, the painter! Isn't this where she is hiding from the world?"

I couldn't speak. I couldn't think.

"I'm terribly sorry I'm late!" she continued. "But you see, I went to the wrong house and you probably won't believe this, but there was some kind of orgy going on over there! And of course, I couldn't help peeping! Who can blame me?"

The truth slowly dawned on me and I started to laugh.

I kissed the ground.

I inhaled the fragrance of the earth.

I saluted my friends the old oak trees who whispered:
*"The time has come baby girl, the time has come ..."*

And then I slowly rose to my feet.

Catherine Colbert handed me a pink paper tissue from her Louis Vuitton city leather bag.

"You look like you are in a state of shock, girl!" she said. "And, by the way, you are naked! Well, of course you are naked, you´re the model, aren't you? The gorgeous one!"

She smiled, delighted:

"I just had to come and see her latest masterpiece! Did I come at a bad time?"

I smiled back at her:

"No, believe it or not, your timing couldn't be better! Come with me! Let me show you the love of my life!"

**\*\*\* The End \*\*\***

# "The Event"

**M**izkaol is posing in front of the mirror again, dressed in the red uniform.

I watch my brother for a long time and suddenly I hate him. Not for being so handsome, or for being so much in lust with his own reflection. I hate him for being invited to The Event just because he is male.

It's obvious that Mizkaol is not in love with Zaphyria Cel'Ador.

But judging from all the poses and acting in front of the mirror he might very well be in love with the challenge of her Event.

Zaphyria Cel'Ador is the only surviving child of our old ruler, and being invited to one of her Events is the greatest honor any young man in our colony can receive.

The Events are surrounded by the utmost secrecy and nobody outside the immediate family must ever find out that my brother has been chosen to participate.

The pledge of silence is something Mother finds almost unbearable.

When Mizkaol leaves the room I lock the door and take out the picture of Zaphyria from the box in the closet where he hides his pleasure herbs and the precious Letter of Invitation.

I will never get used to how insanely beautiful she is, no matter how many times I look at the picture. Zaphyria's hair is black like a winter's night and so long and untamed it might as well strangle you, as shelter you from the chill of the world. The fire in her brown eyes is so welcoming it makes my skin tingle. But in the centre of the fire where nobody dares to venture, I detect something so cold it makes me fear for the sanity of us both.

Spilled out next to me on my brother's bed, abandoned like a bodiless skin, with the color of fresh dark blood, lies the handsome uniform.

I close my eyes and caress it tenderly and it feels just like the soft fur of tiny kittens against my palm.

I whisper:

"I love you Zaphyria. Oh, I love you more than life itself!"

My throat hurts as if I had swallowed fire sticks and I feel miserable.

Why him?

Why not me?

Then I try it on; the false skin of manhood, the armor of bravery, soaked in the color of fresh blood.

The red uniform has tiny buttons and hooks and straps everywhere to make the chosen body beneath it appear as masculine as possible. It flattens my chest and provides a little extra padding over the shoulders and arms.

Mizkaol has explained to me the purpose of the hood and the mask. For mysterious reasons known only to Zaphyria Cel'Ador, the young men must not recognize each other before, during or after The Event, and hence the mask.

When I pull down the mask it clings to my face like a second skin that reveals no emotions. It covers all of my face except for my mouth, nostrils and my eyes, and it hardens the features.

I look at myself in the mirror. With my long red blonde hair and girl's face hidden under the hood and the mask I might be mistaken for a young man.

I have to look again.

How handsome he is, the young man in front of me! How bravely his young heart beats when he looks into my eyes and declares:

"I would give my life for you, Zaphyria. "

When I leave the house at moonrise my brother is safely locked inside his room and sound asleep, thanks to the pleasure herbs I have put in his tea. The Spix-of-the-Wounded root-concoction Mother uses against evil spirits has swelled my throat and made my voice darker.

At the time and place stated in the Letter of Invitation, Instructor Silver arrives to pick me up, in a golden barouche driven by four white Magenta thoroughbreds.

I bow to him and the magnificent horses and hand over the Letter of Invitation.

The old man opens the door to the golden barouche with a hairy wrinkled hand. I step inside and take a seat among five young men all dressed in beautiful red uniforms with their heads and faces covered by the hood and mask attached to the uniform.

We nod to each other but are careful not to talk, since we are prohibited to reveal our identities.

Two hours later we pass the high iron gates of the old Castle of Zeba's Tribe. Instructor Silver smiles for the first time, but his smile is very far from his cold yellow eyes when he says:

"I advise you to follow me closely. You all know the history of this castle and its secret gardens, don't you?"

I do and that's why I am careful not to look anywhere but on Instructor Silver's lead boots as we climb up the steep hill.

We enter the magnificent castle trough a dark high hall, lit by torches only. Deep scratch marks on the high walls make me think of a frantic giant bird desperately trying to claw its way out, to escape the horrors and whims of this infamous castle and its owners.

Strange sounds penetrate the thick walls. It's the wails from the chained guardian dogs somewhere very close, and their growls and wailings from starvation rage and misery; and the rustle from their chains, magnified by the acoustics of the stone castle, makes me feel sick to my stomach.

Suddenly and out of nowhere we are surrounded by a flock of birds. They attack us furiously with their wings and beaks as if we have interrupted them in their ancient sleep. I forget that I am supposed to be a courageous young man, and throw myself on the cold stone floor.

I have never felt so helpless in my entire life, nor have I ever behaved so cowardly.

When the violent birds have disappeared, chased away by a huge albino Baziba-hawk, the young men gaze around the walls triumphantly, as if they believe that somewhere behind the cold stones, the mistress of Castle of Zeba's Tribe herself might be watching them, admiring their courage and handsome young bodies.

Instructor Silver approaches us with six sheets of paper and six golden pens on a golden tray. He bows to us:

"Bear in mind when you answer The Question that She-Who-is-Designated-to-Be-One-With-All-Power attaches equally importance to the mind of the heart and the heart of the mind."

While the young men twitch uncomfortably at the sound of his words I touch the white document, and eagerly, thirsty for a glimpse of my beloved's mind, I read The Question:

*"WHERE DO YOU HIDE YOUR FEAR?"*

I don't even have to think before I answer:

*I wear my fear like an armor to protect me against life. Life is nothing without love and love is the only life I have got inside me."*

Instructor Silver collects our sheets of paper and we are left to wait for a long time. We sit on the cold floor with nothing else to do than tending to our bird bite wounds and wipe off the red BloodBeeze, thirsty for a sip of blood from a Human youth. When Inspector Silver returns he points at me:

"You! This way!"

I'm escorted into a room with a high arched ceiling, with the color of the sky at the hesitation of dawn. The walls are adorned with ancient tapestries the same rich red, green and blue color as the soft velvety rugs on the marble floor. Fragrances from the Essenceina Orchard is sipping in through the open windows overlooking the Silver Lake and three of the Moon Gardens and blends with the fragrance of thousands of freshly cut flowers in ancient urns, placed around the blue walls.

This room is more beautiful than anything I could ever have imagined, but what is really breathtaking is she.

Somewhere far back in the shadows, among the tapestries and flowers, she is watching me as I make my entrance.

Zaphyria Cel'Ador is dressed in a long dress, blue as the night skies reflected in the deep ocean, soft and weightless as the clouds, shiny as pale moonlight. I can see the contours of her body through the thin layers of blue fabric like a pale seashell through layers of water.

Her long black hair reaches down to her waist and the soft breeze from outside makes it move a little.

Suddenly I feel like I'm being pierced by death while looking into the sun. Her beauty terrifies me.

My innocence is not by choice. My love is of the kind that is so rare I have only heard it spoken of once, and not kindly. What I feel now is unworthy of me and of my love for her, and unworthy of the beautiful red uniform I am wearing in her honor. But the terror of this moment makes me fear I will faint, from feelings too strong for any human being to endure.

I stretch out my trembling hand but she ignores it.

"Take it off!" she orders.

I look at my hand and suddenly I don't understand. Her voice is dark and void of emotion.

"Your mask!" she demands, impatiently, as if I am very old, or very young, or have a very slow mind. "Well? Take-it-off!"

I shake my head, unable to think.

She stares at me.

"Are you refusing to obey my order? How dare you?"

"I am not beautiful." I say, and my voice is trembling.

"*Beautiful?*"

She tastes the word curiously, like I have offered her a strange fruit. Then she replies.

"Keep it on, then! I'll just have to pretend that you are ... beautiful. How I wish I had chosen somebody else. Somebody beau-ti-ful! To expel my darkness!"

Her brown eyes are dark with rage and disappointment, and the way she uses the word beautiful makes it sound as an obscenity, or a curse.

Suddenly I feel miserable for deceiving her and making her so disappointed, so I whisper:

"It's not too late."

Zaphyria is silent again, as if she cannot believe I answered her back. Then she says:

"I could have you whipped for that comment!"

"*Oh...!*"

"You are so rude ....!"

She draws her breath:

"... so rude it's almost amusing!"

I am so nervous that I have to cough.

She notices how nervous I am and she laughs.

"Un-beautiful one!"

"Yes?"

"Didn't they prepare you for the etiquette and protocol on the Night of My Event?"

"Y-yes..."

I have no idea what she is talking about. Mizkaol never told me about this part.

"And-..? And-..? And-..?" she says impatiently, waving her hand to make me talk.

"Yes..." I lie. "They...prepared me."

I try to swallow the lump in my throat. She waits for me to say something, but my mind is still blank, so, finally she adds; her voice softer, inquisitive; curious almost:

"You really don't know, do you?"

I shake my head.

"So tell me; what do you do?"

"D-d-do?"

"Can you sing like a castrato?"

"N-no..."

"Can you eat fire?"

"N-no."

"Can you juggle with broken glass?"

"No...!"

"Can you recite *the big Bloma's sixty-six hymns to passion*, balancing on an empty wine barrel, hands tied behind your back?"

"No-o...!"

"Can you walk on your hands with the blade of a dagger inside your mouth?"

"N-no..!"

"Can you put your feet behind your neck and continue a conversation and still look dignified?"

"No...."

"Can you keep your breath under polluted water for four minutes?"

"No."

"Can you stick rusty needles under your nails without uttering a sound?"

"No!"

"Can you wrestle my mad guardian dogs King and Queen for half an hour?"

"No!"

"Can you drink the month-old moon blood of fifty hegans in one sip?"

"No."

She makes a deep sigh and makes some impatient movements with her arms.

"You bore me to death. And not even fifteen minutes have passed on this endless night of endless boredom."

"It feels like an eternity!" I agree silently.

My voice is feeble because my heart is beating like a frantic bird imprisoned behind the ribs of my chest. She stares at me; her brown eyes burning with fury, and flashes of fiery ice blind me, as I try to meet her gaze, unable to move.

The sudden blow knocks out all the air out of my lungs as I fall backwards and land on my arm. When I open my eyes I can't breathe because I am in so much pain. She is leaning over me.

"So you ... dare telling me that I... that I bore... you?"

"No..."

"You rude son of a nothing of a nothing of a shit eating fly! Apologize! Immediately! On your knees!"

Somehow I manage to turn around to the side, trying to get up on my knees, but my arm hurts so much I can taste blood, and without thinking I reach out to lean on her shoulder for support, grasping the front of her thin blue dress, and there is a sharp, ominous sound of torn fabric.

I can't believe what I have done and what I now see in front of me.

"I'm sorry ... I'm sorry...!"

I fall back on the floor without being able to take my eyes off her breasts. They are perfectly shaped and more lovely than anything I have ever seen in my life. My hands ache so much from the desire to touch the soft skin of her breasts I could cry.

"You are staring at my breasts!" she gasps.

"*Yes...*" I sigh, breathless, paralyzed by pain and beauty.

She sits there, close to me, confident, curious almost, legs slightly apart in a very unladylike manner, observing me as I stare at her exposed breasts.

"You are different from the rest, you know." She says.

"Not much. Just a little. Insignificant and little, just like you. But different, still."

The she goes on talking, and it sounds like she is talking to herself.

"They all use me. They are prepared to do anything, just anything to make me fall for them so they can steal what I will soon possess."

I am still dizzy from the fall and from the pain in my shoulder and arm, and my eyes are transfixed on her breasts so close to me, so close to my hands, so I mumble in a haze of confusion:

"Steal your *breasts?*"

She looks at me, unable to reply, and starts to laugh. And the laughter makes her shake, and then she gets a grip on herself, and kicks me with her tiny white suede ankle boot. It's not a hard kick but not a soft kick either.

Nobody has ever kicked me before, not even Mizkaol when we were children, and I don't like it.

"So tell me!" she yells. "What do you want from me, you filth-worm, you shit-head, you piece of worthless replaceable merchandise? A job in the Fifth Division? A mansion at the end of Digmy?"

I can't believe my ears. I can't believe that somebody as beautiful as Zaphyria can use such foul language. Mother told me once that only very sad people use foul language. And if I would ever meet such a person I must be very kind to them because they carry the worm of death inside their hearts.
So I ask her kindly:

"Do you have many friends, Zaphyria?"

"Friends!? What do I need friends for? To bore me to death with their mindless chatter?
She makes a cruel imitation of a group of women chatting and her long white hands moves in the air like the small wings of a bird when she talks; and suddenly I feel as if they are all over me, moving inside me, touching me everywhere, and I can no longer take my eyes off her beautiful hands.

"Whom do you share your inner thoughts with?" I whisper.
My throat is thick with these exquisite emotions I can't understand because I have never felt them before. But now I can feel them everywhere in my body, like a sweet ache, almost like a hunger, starving for closeness to the mirror of my own flesh.

"I don't want to share my things!" she says. "Least of all my inner thoughts! And never with any of your kind!" She watches me for a second and then volunteers:

"I just meet with you men for a few hours. I humiliate you as much I as I can, but never as much as you deserve. I watch you all trying so hard to please me. To charm me. To impress me with your courage. Nobody has ever succeeded. Nobody ever will."

When she laughs it's a strange, ragged laugh, not like a laugh at all. It sounds more like a distorted sob, from a stifled cry.

"At the end of The Event you will get exhausted and desperate and pay me more insipid compliments. And afterwards you will go and beat up some poor woman somewhere in NeuwGaina, and pretend she is I. But I know you better than you know yourselves. I have you all calculated and I am smarter than the six of you put together with the sixty before you."

She shakes her head as in disbelief and adds:

"And still … still, every single one of you believe that you are infinitely superior to me!"

"But why then do you have these Events?"

She looks at me directly now with a big frown on her forehead.

"*Why*? You know the big why!"

"No."

Whereupon she clenches her fists and screams to me at the top of her voice as if I am deaf:

"Because I must marry one of you!"

"But Zaphyria; you are soon to be the most powerful one in the entire Blir. And then who will dare telling you what you can, or cannot do?"
She looks at me as if she doesn't know if I am just plain stupid, or if I am trying to make her appear so:

"Ha! Later, when I have crushed your inflated ego, ugly-boy, you will please me with your mouth!"

"Flatter you, you mean?"
At first she is silent for a long time, and then she laughs again, but this time amused, like I had said something immensely, almost incredibly funny:

"You know, un-beautiful, inquisitive coward-boy, I have never told anyone this before, man or woman: I act. All the time."

"Me too, Zaphyria."
I want to touch her hand. The bird in its blood calls for my touch.

"But of course you do! Good with words, you are, and that's why I chose you among the crowd of imbeciles, but a spineless coward and a lousy actor and you move like a scared puppy. I could tell you wanted to hit me a little while ago!"
She throws her head back and giggles.

"No! Never! I don't like violence!"

"Of course you like it!" she says. "Like the rest of them you love to inflict harm on all living things!"

"I would never harm you, Zaphyria! I'm different!" I whisper.

She laughs, very amused and moves closer to me to observe me, as I lay there helpless and aching because of what she has done to my heart and body.

"You love power, don't you; the power to conquer, to possess, to dominate; bodies, minds, souls. And what am I, to each and every one of you? ... Just a thing, a symbol, another valuable possession ... something to be conquered, possessed, dominated and handed over; mind, body and soul, to another one of you ...!"

Her voice breaks down and she starts to hit me with her fist on my chest. Her long black hair assists her in her endeavors. I have never seen anyone so sad in my entire life. I have only seen Mother cry once, when Father left with the Third Division for SpeKychia, but Mother's sadness was mixed with pride and happiness.

Suddenly I realize that my own sufferings are nothing compared to Zaphyria's.

I can feel her unhappiness burn on my skin like sparks of fire. Her pain is unbearable to me; the fire that is consuming her scorches me. Before she can protest, I grab her arms with all the force I am mighty of, and I press her down to the floor. And then I silence her with my mouth. Her lips are even softer than I had imagined. An arrow of heat penetrates my heart and my private parts, and it turns into the hot sweet pain, the fiery nectar of her eyes. It feels so good I almost faint.

She gasps.

"How dare you!"

"You are so sad. Somebody hurt you, didn't they?"

"And what makes you any different?" she spits. "You are rude and insolent and refuse to obey my orders, and look what you did to my dress!"

"I am different!"

"You are all the same to me ... so why... why... why...must I continue... this *charade*, this *pretence*, this endless *play* with empty words?"

I can't support myself on my shoulder long enough to get up from her because it hurts too much, and I know I should be ashamed for my inexcusable behavior, and I know I must be insane, but lying there on top of her between her legs, I am filled with so much happiness and such exquisite feelings I could die, and each time I try to move away from her, I fail, and push against her instead, and she starts to move her head and bite her lip, as if my movements make her insane, too.

"Don't look at me!" she moans.

She is flushed in her face and her pupils are dark. She arches her back and her breasts press against the chest of my red uniform, and her stiff little buds push against my soft uniform, like they want to penetrate it.

"Make me laugh. Or make me come!"

"Come? But ... but ... You are already here...?"

She starts to laugh her strange laugh that sounds more like crying, and I can see a small teardrop running down her left cheek.

"Kiss me again!" she says, almost out of breath.

"I like your lips, and your breath. Let me pretend ... things ..."

She kisses me again, like I am a little stream of water and she is dying from thirst and wants to suck me dry. Her tongue speaks to mine in a language of the blood I'm not familiar with, and I feel dizzy, like I am going to faint, like I'm melting, my centre is turning moist and liquid.

Then abruptly, she tears herself from my lips, rolls over on her side, and spits:

"I don't like ... *men.*"

She dries her lips on her sleeve, suddenly disgusted with me and with herself.

"But I do!" I confess, I protest, thinking of my brother, annoying, as he might be most of the time, but wonderful also, and sweet and always so much fun. And I remember my father with his red beard; big and kind to all living things, and his deep, happy laughter; always so full of surprises, always, always, my beloved Father.

"Of course you adore men! You are one!"

"Sorry, I-I-I forgot..."

"Forgot...? How can anybody, anywhere, anytime forget something like that? It's the only thing that matters!"

"No. Love is the only thing that matters." I say.

She starts to laugh again for a long time and this time her laughter is spiteful.

"Love ... love ... love... Ha! I bet your organ is the size of a peanut! Take off you mask, now, you pathetic little worm!"

"No!"

"I am sick and tired of your game and your appalling mask!"

"Please, no!"

"I order you! Do it! Now!" she screams at the top of her voice.

"Please, Zaphyria, please, please... don't!" I beg her. She hesitates. Confused.

"No ...no... no...!" I whisper. "Please....!"

She lies on the floor supported by her arms with her legs apart and her breasts exposed and the cruel look on her face has turned into an expression I can't interpret, as if she is possessed by a fever or an itch or something that is so painful it feels good:

"But I implore you, mysterious one!" she says, out of breath and in pain, consumed by a feverish madness I have never heard of, as if she wants to eat me or die in me, and hasn't made up her mind, yet.

I slowly remove the hood and the mask from my face and my long red blond locks fall down my shoulders in heavy waves.

First she gives out a small cry. Then she remains silent and motionless for a long time and she looks at me with so much hatred in her eyes I have to look away.

When she finally addresses me, her voice is toneless:

"Have you any idea what you have done to me? How much you have humiliated me?"

"No..." I whisper.

"No? Why did you come here? As some kind of a morbid punishment, just to increase my sufferings?"
She grabs my shoulders and shakes me.

"Why? Why? Why?" she cries.

"I hide my wings in you; I can feel their shadow move in me, forever."
She covers her face in her hands and starts to moan, as if I had hit her.

"What are you talking about?"

"I love you Zaphyria …" I whisper.
At my words she screams like I had turned a knife in her heart.

"I could have you executed for this!"
Her brown eyes are glowing. She is so beautiful the sunset is intimidated by the comparison.

"Yes. Yes, I know you will." I say.
She stops moaning, and just stares at me, lips slightly parted.

"What's your name, insolent one?"

"Vilja Valouria …"

"Vilja Valouria, tell me something; when you came here, with the intentions of humiliating me … didn't you know what the consequences of your actions would be?"

"Yes, that was the only thing I was certain of." I whisper.

Ever since I stole my brother's uniform I have known that I would die for love: for never knowing it, or for knowing it once. But never could I have imagined that death itself would terrify me so.

Perhaps it is because I am too young to die....
Oh, Mother, Father, sweet Brother of mine...
What have I done...?
I am terrified of death.
But I will not cry because I have tasted those soft lips
and the nectar of her mouth. I have felt her body close to
mine and have felt things too wondrous for words.
Love.
I will not cry in front of her.

Zaphyria is watching me for the longest time. I am
surprised to see that her eyes are filled with tears.
　　"Don't cry! I know you must kill me." I say.

I'm not yet dead but my body is cold and my voice has
lost the light of life.
　　I hope the execution will take place in the old
dungeons of death. I hope that death will be quick and
she will let my body disappear without any trace.
Perhaps she will feed me to the starving dogs ...

　　"Vilja Valouria, listen to me! You are the bravest soul
I have ever met! But before tonight I never understood
the magnitude of my power!"
　　"*No?*" My voice sounds dry, like the flight of dead
leaves in a storm.
　　"No. I have always been a stranger to love, the power
of love and the insane sacrifices of love."
　　"So where?" I ask.

My voice is the voice of a ghost and I wish, I pray, I hope that her beautiful face and the fire of her sad brown eyes will be the last thing I see before I enter the black winter's night of death.

"Where ... *what?*" she asks.

"Where will you take me, Zaphyria?"

A shy smile plays on Zaphyria trembling lips.

"Vilja Valouria- ..." she whispers, her voice thick with emotions and as tender as mother's hand on her newborn child. "...will you please come with me to bed and make me yours, you lovely, lovely girl?"

The Beginning

## "Pink Magic"

**We** were six at first; Dylan, Tishy, Keith, Mike, Selebrity and me. It was my birthday and since they knew how much I hated fairs they took me to one, blindfolded of course so I wouldn't know until it was too late.

That's how they were, back then. And that's how they remained. I guess that's why I still love them after all these years; those selfish, genius, gallant goofs who wanted to give med the best birthday ever, and - did.

I confess I might have had a little sip too many of a little liquid something in the car, and just maybe, just maybe, I might have inhaled a little fume from a little something too, but, honestly, I was blindfolded, and besides I kept yelling it was my birthday, so maybe that's why they kept stuffing things into my mouth?

And being the star of the event and a perfect hostess I made sure that everyone was properly entertained and burped a little *"Happy Birthday to Me"*- song to show my sincere appreciation and help elevate the mood to an even higher state of bliss.

Birthdays can be so much fun.

That was until Dylan decided to make his own musical contribution and started to fart. But I prefer to forget that part. And besides by then we were almost there. When the car stopped all six passengers in the car, and especially the four of us in the back, were desperate to get to the fair.

Thanks to Dylan.

Selebrity was sitting next to me in the car and I just loved the thrill of feeling her long pink fingernails on my back when we fell out of the car.

Selebrity has always had an exquisite sense of style. So refined was her taste even back then, that the color of her fingernails matched the color of her panties. But only I knew this, (and possibly Keith). Her panties were pink with tiny butterflies, and how I envied those butterflies. All over her butt, they were. And shameless, too.

Interior monologue falling out of car:

"What would you like to be in your next life young woman?"

"Thank you for asking; divine fulfiller of all crazy wishes, a.k.a. genie spirit of the whisky bottle. I would like to be one of the butterflies on the pink cotton underwear that Selebrity Hanson wears."

"What are you laughing at?" Selebrity asked, hands still on my back. "You crazy, crazy woman!"

"Yummy, yummy, yummy I've got love in my tummy!" I sang at the top of my voice.

"Perv'!"

"No I'm serious!"

"Yeah, and we all know he loves you, too." Selebrity said sourly.

At that moment I started to get sick. Sad-sick. The worst kind of sick.

My sadistically inclined friends had made me wear this silly T-shirt with some homemade letters glued to the chest. Since I was blindfolded I couldn't see what message I was promoting, but everybody we passed howled or shouted things like *"Good Luck, Lady"*. And to this day I still have no clue as to what it said on the T-shirt because to this day they still refuse to tell me. They just grin and say; "Well, wouldn't you like to know?"

Selebrity told the guys that she and I would be back in a moment due to some unexpected events pertaining to the female body, and they didn't object.

Only Dylan objected a little but mainly because he didn't understand what she said.

Selebrity and I bumped into a lot of people, or, I did, until she decided to remove my blindfold. By then people were starting to lose their sense of humor as rapidly as I started to lose my sense of directions, particular north and south, and I was starting to feel sick, and who knows whom I might have ended up offending, be it in the east or west direction, if I had kept the blindfold on.

All the time Selebrity's soft hands were on my back supporting me. I could feel those long pink fingernails through the back of my thin T-shirt like a reminder of some adult aspects of life I hoped soon to be explored.

It was then she said those horrible words.

"You and I will always be best friends, Mona."

I couldn't reply because I was squatting, throwing up. My head was spinning. I felt like an insect. A very heavy, very green one. Filled with fumy pesticides aimed to humiliate me to death. Locked forever inside a huge vibrating vacuum cleaner that kept pressing my tummy together, buzzing the words friends, friends, friends.

"*What a shitty thing to say!*" I thought. "*And on my birthday, too!*"

Next thing I knew she slapped me on my back. And yelled:

"Why did you say that?"

"Say what...?"

"You said: "*What a shitty thing to do on my birthday ...!*"

"No..."

"Did you really think I wanted you to get sick? And barf? On your birthday?"

She looked so unhappy I couldn't help but laugh, and say:

"Who knows what goes on inside that sick head of yours, woman? I bet you wanted me all sick and helpless so you could touch my bazookas!"

I expected her to play along, and deliver a really mean one-liner, like she always did, but instead she turned bright read.

"You're so gross sometimes. Just like a man!" She said.

And she sounded exactly like Hillary, her mother.

"Yeah? So? You like men, don't you?"

"Of course I do; don't you, Mona?"

"Do you even need to ask?"

I grinned. She grinned back. Like two participants in some mean grinning contest. And then suddenly the air stopped breathing us and we both stopped grinning.

In the middle of this confusion the weather wizard decided to play a little trick on us, to force us to grow up, I guess. When it started to rain the letters of my T-shirt started falling off before I got a chance to read what they said.

I felt faint for more reasons than I cared to think about, and needed to sit down somewhere, and Selebrity didn't want to ruin her new experimental hairstyle that she had spent the whole day preparing.

So Selebrity pointed somewhere up the dirt road, and somewhere over the brink of the pink fingernail of her index finger I discovered a small white tent. She took me by the hand and led me astray (I hoped) and after a few sweet minutes of running and holding hands she dragged me inside.

The tent was crowded with people. Small kerosene lanterns placed on two long wooden tables were the only sources of light. People were sitting around the wooden tables or standing in small groups laughing and shouting. They were all dressed up in bright clothes, and looked a bit like circus people from old black-and-white movies (except in color). It wasn't just the clothes that seemed strange, but their bodies and faces, too. They were all sizes and shapes. One of them had two heads and one in his pocket.

(Or maybe I wasn't quite sober, yet).

We sat down next to a bearded lady and a small monkey, and looked around. I still felt faint and dizzy, but the monkey wore a red vest and a little hat and was really cute.

The monkey gave me some peanuts and I said "*Thank you, dear!*" and Selebrity said "Ooooh how polite!" and I said "*Thank you, dear!*" again and Selebrity said "*Not you, silly!*" and the monkey bowed and a man with real horns on his forehead and huge biceps laughed so much he spilled half of his beer on the ground.

"Finally! There you are!"

A woman my mother's age, in her late forties, early nineties, approached us. She had long curly dark red hair down to her waist and wore huge earrings in gold and was dressed in a green skirt with gazillions of shawls around her waist and neck and tons of clicking silver bracelets around her arms. She had more makeup on her face and perfume on her body than my mother uses for a whole month, and sparkled like a man-magnet, or a sun-wannabee.

For some reason she looked really upset and the silver bracelets around her arms made a lot of clicking noises because she was speaking with her entire body, waving her arms and staring at us furiously as if we had told her old people belong in a zoo or should be banned from public beaches, or should only be allowed 200 calories a day, or something really offensive.

"Where have you been?"

"What?" Selebrity and I looked at each other and made some funny faces behind our hands. (Our today's special; "*What mental asylum did she escape from-faces.*")

"I have been looking all over for you!"

Selebrity made some delicious snorting noises through her delicious nose and I banged my head on the table.

"Come on! You can't sit here! Come on, come on, come on! You have to get dressed!"

"Yes, Ma'am!" We said, Selebrity and I, the discipline of our strict mothers ingrained in our backbones like an ugly irremovable socially inherited disease.

We rose and followed the lady, staggering, suffocating with oppresses laughter, unable to utter a word. My heart ached with love. So the guys were hiding somewhere, planning to give me my best ever birthday surprise. Was I ever lucky to have such friends!

I was truly impressed by the way Selebrity could keep her poker face, and very curious about the big surprise. This took some serious planning to execute, and planning wasn't their strong side, I mean Dylan couldn't plan his toilet visits some days, so I was truly flattered. This was so freaking adult!

Selebrity was giving me long, secret glances in order to read my reaction to the surprise scheme, while I tried to keep my face straight.

"You can change in there!" said the lady and opened the door to a small trailer.


We stepped inside and looked around the small room. The black walls were covered in veils and artificial spider webs and gilded mirrors and lit candles, and unfocused black-and–white photos of smoky, ghostlike people were pinned to the walls. Two piles of strange colorful clothes were placed on two small chairs.

"Hurry!" the lady said. "Five minutes to go! People are expecting you!"

She clapped her hands and Selebrity and I started to undress, still giggling.

The black velvet dress fit me perfectly and the blouse that went with it was a dream of white lace. Before Selebrity had put on her beautiful burgundy velvet dress and black lace blouse I had a few delicious moments to admire her delicious pink butterfly panties, and she turned red again.

"Mona! Stop it! I have a dozen. Don't look at me like that!" She screamed.

The lady entered the trailer.

"If you are good and pass the test I will grant each of you a wish!" she said.

"Ok." I said. "Great. What kind of a wish!"

"Best kind there is. Love kind."

She smiled and rolled her eyes. Then she held her clenched fists in front of her and asked:

"In which hand do I hold the rings?"

I pointed at one of her hands and Selebrity pointed at the other, and the lady opened her hands and we were both right. The lady gave them to us, and we put them on our ring fingers. She laughed.

"For protection! And magic!" she said and sounded very much like my own mother, lately. (Except for the magic part).

The lady laughed again. "Props!"

The lady led us outside, downhill, on a small dirt road, even further away from the fair, and finally we came to an open space with a small hill, where we climbed up a few steps to a small circular stage. Somewhere in the dark I could hear the mumbling of voices close by.

Suddenly the light from at least a hundred simultaneously lit torches were blinding us, shining in our faces, and we couldn't see the crowd surrounding us below, just hear their mumbling. I tried to discern the voices of Mike, Dylan, Tishy, and Keith, generously sharing their own particular sense of humour with the world, by delivering unbelievably immature and goofy one-liners, but couldn't hear them.

Their command of self-discipline surprised me immensely and impressed me even more, because Selebrity and I were really something to behold that night on that small stage below the stars.

Selebrity gave me some furtive glances; actually she looked a little bit worried. Maybe the guys hadn't filled her in on this part. I smiled back.

"Just enjoy!" I whispered.

"Do you?"

"Yeah!"

"And by the way; thanks!" I said.

"For what?" she said.

"For this! For being such a great actress!" I said.

She gave me a look I couldn't interpret. Like if she didn't know if she should enjoy the compliment, or not.

"It takes one to know one!" she finally said.

Gigantic flames surrounded us, roaring, hot and scorching, too close for comfort, even licking at our feet, now and then.

The crowd started to applaud and cheer. We could hear drums. The flames prevented us from seeing the crowd below the stage but it was exciting in a scary way, and Selebrity and I were in the centre of all the attention.

"*Women warriors of the Sky, join us!*" the lady chanted.

"*Join us, join us!*" the crowd repeated.

We looked intensely but could not see anyone or anything descending from the sky.

"Look inside yourselves!" they shouted.

"This is just too much!" I said to Selebrity and giggled.

"Yes, this is all so you." She said. "Too much!"

Suddenly the lady was next to us on the stage.

"Repeat!" the lady told us waving her arms shawls floating in the air like a big insane bird, the bracelets around her arms making clicking sounds like a foreign instrument. "You must repeat!"

"Repeat?" I asked. "Repeat what?"

"Take each other by the wrist, look each other in the eyes, dance inside the circle and repeat!"

So Selebrity and I did as told, skipped around the boards, chanting "Join us, Women Warriors of the Sky, join us", giggling like crazy.

"Now stop!"

So we stopped.

If I had been a guy, or rather, if I had been Keith, I would have kissed her there and then. Because that would have been the perfect moment to kiss Selebrity Hanson.

She looked so beautiful, enlightened by the torches, dressed in her burgundy velvet dress with the little black and green embroideries everywhere and her special hairdo with frizzles and gems and purple and green stuff and her cute nose and soft lips and the look in those big brown eyes, that new look that made me all dizzy and happy and sad and ...

At that moment, that second moment of magic confusion the same night, someone threw a torch on the stage. Not even Dylan on an off-medication day would do anything as reckless.

We both screamed when it scorched my dress.

"Shit, Mona, I'm scared!"
Selebrity clung to me but unfortunately I was too scared myself to fully enjoy the intimacy.

"Don't be. They won't let anything harm us!" I said, trying to sound calm, but failing.

The crowd started to hum. The torch had set the planks on the stage on fire and the roaring of the flames and the heat was truly frightening now.

The lady was next to us again waving her shawls among the flames like a madwoman.

"Seek deliverance!" the lady shouted.

"What? Where?" I screamed.

"Seek deliverance beneath, between, and within yourselves!" the lady shouted.

"Don't just stand there – do something!"

She sounded so much like my mother, and I suddenly realized the bird lady was talking about directions and looked down on the boards and discovered that Selebrity and I were standing on a door, hidden under the dirt like the door to a storm cellar.

I found the iron door-handle and jerked it open and grabbed Selebrity's hand. We had no time to peek inside, or to hesitate even for a second, before we took a step out in the air and jumped, first Selebrity and then I.

Selebrity and I landed on hard soil, confused, scared, bruised and coughing, but alive. And then the storm cellar door closed above our heads with a loud boom, like a furious omen of some kind.

And who was waiting for us down there?

Standing there, just smiling?

No. Not Mike, Dylan, Tishy, or Keith, but the weird shawl lady holding a burning torch in her hand. She must have taken another door to the cellar below the stage. Maybe Selebrity and I had fainted for a few minutes as we hit planet earth again, or the lady must have been moving at the speed of light.

"Now the two of you are properly cleansed from the ignorance of the surface!" the lady said.

We couldn't laugh this time. Selebrity was shaking, and I guess I was too. We had barely made it. A few minutes later and we would have been dead, consumed by the flames. What a sad way to go. And on your birthday, too.

"Thank you for making me jump!" Selebrity said, in her tiniest voice.

"I had to. Sorry if I had to be a little rough on you. But you are such a coward, baby." I said. I tried to sound casual but didn't succeed. My voice was thick with emotions.

Selebrity didn't reply. Just blushed again. Shaking and blushing, she was. And her new special hairstyle all in a mess now, too.

"How come you sound so different? So mature?" she said. "You are only one day older?"

"Actually I am a year older. Seventeen, and believe me, it makes all the difference."

I could tell by the look in her eyes she believed me.

The woman looked at us and opened her big bag.

"I have got your reward here."

I looked at Selebrity and she looked at me. We looked at the cookies in the lady's hand. They looked just like any old cookies. Except these were glowing pink and radiating like they had been excavated from some abandoned nuclear plant in Eastern Europe.

And I shrugged my shoulders.

"Why not, or what do you say, Seal-ee?"

"Well if you say so, Mon-ee." She said.

"It is a love potion, or, if you like, a truth serum. If the one you love is thinking of you when you eat it you will find love and be forever in love."

"And - if not?" I asked, my tummy in an uproar.

"Well, you can always return next year." The woman said.

Selebrity and I took a bite at our cookies and looked at each other.

"I know who you are thinking of." Selebrity said, and then she looked sad all of a sudden.

"No, I guarantee you don't." I said. "But I know who you are thinking of."

"No, you can't. You are the brainiest person I know but you still have no clue."

We ate our cookies but didn't look at each other. They tasted like dry old teabags and made my eyes tear up.

"Come on, guys! Don't look so sad!" the lady said. "This is supposed to be fun!"

"But how will we know if it works?" I asked.

"I will give each of you a special question. Later you must ask the person of your dreams that special question and if the person is the right person you will see a little pink star emerge on their cheek."

"Magic!" I said, with my Special Squeaky Cartoon Animal Voice.

"Cool!" said Selebrity, but her own voice was a scared and sad little voice, just pretending to enjoy this fairy variation of Truth of Dare.

And all of a sudden I felt so sad. I suddenly felt grown up in the non-magical sort of a way, in that "what are the odds of winning one million dollars when you haven't even bought a lottery ticket" sort of a sad way.

And then the lady whispered the special question in our ears, one at the time.

"Don't forget the question, now!" she said. "And remember, it can only be used one time, and only on one person, mind you! And if you can see a little pink star on the cheek of that person, you will know that person will love you forever."

She grinned a very big grin to both of us, and there was a new expression in her eyes.

"Come on, you two! I know young people!" she smiled. "Always in love with love!"

And she clasped her hands, shook her head and sighed.

"Yeah. Aren't we just freaking adorable?" Selebrity said; her voice filled with so much irony I just stared at her.

"You two are more than just adorable, believe me!" the woman said in a throaty voice, looking at us as if we were two slices of pizza straight out of the oven and she had only been allowed 200 calories a day for the last four days.

"You are welcome to join me later in my trailer. I could teach you one or two things that might come in handy."

Of course I realized that the lady wanted to explore some other fiery aspects of life, most likely in a nudity-related acrobatic sort of a way, but even if I was very old and very curious in lots and lots of ways, I felt that Selebrity and I had had enough excitement for one night, and said:

"Thanks! Maybe we should just go and tell our friends first!"

And off we went, Selebrity and I.

We found Dylan, Tishy, Keith and Mike standing close to a shooting booth stuffing hot dogs into their mouths and pointing guns at some insane looking yellow plastic ducks. We joined the group. I looked at them. They hadn't changed. They wore the same dorky, geek-nerd moron looking expression as always.

"Where have you been?" Mike asked.

"We had some close encounters with real danger!" I said.

"What do you mean ... *exactly* ... like?" Asked Dylan.

"Where was that danger counter place?" Asked Tishy.

"Where did you get those clothes?" Asked Keith.

"Where are birthdays born?" I asked.

"Where do butterfly fly when they die?" Selebrity asked.

"Come-on you guys!" Mike giggled. "Close encounters with real danger? Sure! You went to have some pink girly tattoos. Look at their cheeks!"

That was fifteen years ago today and the memories from that night still make me smile.

Selebrity never became an astronaut, but decided to become a combined hair and nail stylist, and started designing her own brand of clothing inspired by the amazing clothes we decided to keep in return for the jeans and T-shirts we left behind in the weird shawl lady's trailer, and with those three jobs and lots and lots of pink magic she supported us both, and helped me through law school, and somewhere along the line she stopped wearing pink panties with butterflies on, but I forgave her.

The stuff she is wearing now is pure magic too.

**The End**

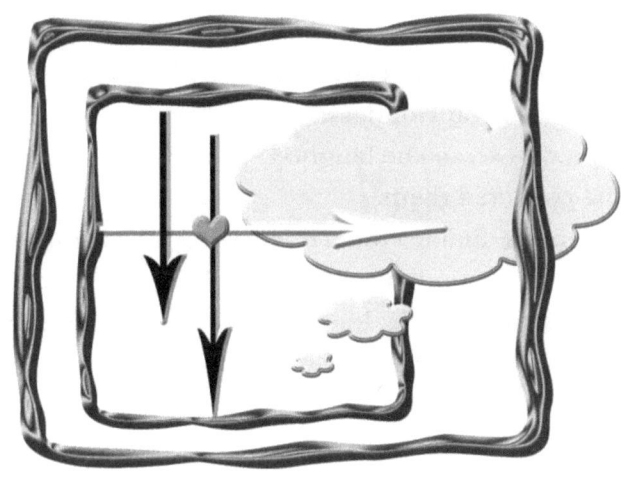

# "The Beholder"

Once upon the time Goddess was bored.

She was bored easily so that wasn't the problem.
The problem was that she was bored with me.

"I really miss you, Earthling." she said.

"But I am always by your side, Goddess."

"Yes. And that is precisely why I miss you."

"I love you Goddess!"

I cried now, so she laughed. She loved my tears so dearly she collected them.

When she finally stopped laughing, she said:

"No, you don't love me. You are becoming me. I miss you. Little human, mortal you. Die, Earthling! Then live, and then we'll see about love...

And then she killed me.

Goddess - being a goddess - had Goddesses matters to attend to.

And Goddess - being a goddess - took her job seriously, (like Dr. Zeus).

When she smiled, the rays of joy entered my darkest corner.

But she didn't.

Goddess, you know I was crying my eyes out.

You left me in the desert.

Alone with my tears and nothing.

And nothing grew in my sadness because the tears were yours to keep.

Dr Zeus had the most exquisite little aura I had ever seen in a mortal.

When surrounded by her chattering colleague-shrinks the colours disappeared completely and she became smaller somehow, greyer, more plain and almost un-distinguishable from anyone out there; she shrunk till the size of a matchbox, - amazing thing to watch it happen! - and her entire being radiated boredom and fatigue and assimilation.

Her entire body closed up, like a top security prison when she was surrounded by her blabbering, jabbering colleagues at the hospital, running in the long corridors like fat mice in a labyrinth, never noticing a thing that went on inside and outside the realms of life, outside their square little heads.

I'm not being patronizing here; the blind shouldn't lead the blind. That's all I say.

I had just made an impersonation of her colleagues "*The Cerebral Zombies*". Just to warm up. It had been so long since I had used words.

(Outside my head that is).

Dr. Zeus smiled sweetly and said:

"Okay. So let's talk about you now, Sche-Hera, and why you are here."

I could tell her interest wasn't entirely professional, so I asked:

"I know you don't believe anything I say. So what's the point, really?"

"Oh, but I *do* believe everything you say, because you *are* telling me the truth, *your* truth.  And that is what I am interested in hearing. Your truth."

"My truth .... my oh my-"

"So tell me again why you are here?" she interrupted.

"Goddess got bored with me."

"Goddess ... got ...bored with you?"

"I am just a human being. I became a pain in her divine rectum – well, metaphorically speaking, that is."

"Are you sure about that?"

"I am here aren't I? What more evidence do you need? She got bored with me, killed me and I woke up in this pathetic parody of hell."

"No, no, no, what I meant was ... Are you absolutely convinced that you are just a human being?"

"What is your professional opinion, Doc? Do I look like a fox or a cow, to you? Or a dog, maybe?"


I was joking.

But she wasn't.

⸻

I admit any day to anyone that having a goddess for a godmother, and a lover, might be considered somewhat unusual, but nevertheless, not sick *per se*. People are as entitled to their secrets, however grand or petty.

Not everyone admits to having been abducted by aliens, either. The social stigma is too great, not to speak of the invisible burns from the engines. Too hard to explain. All of it.

———→

"Why did you shave off your hair?" asked Dr Zeus. "I have seen a picture of you before you ... joined us here at "Lilly Dale's" and you had long beautiful hair."
I smiled and shook my bald head in naked space.

"Goddess did it. You wouldn't understand. It is the only thing that makes me laugh. I liked that stupid hair so much and it still grows on me! All of it! It's a pun, a joke! It's *alive! It's alive!* And I am dead!!"

I started to laugh and I laughed for the longest time. I laughed till my heart ached and it felt so good because I could feel it; I could actually feel the pain of life. I laughed when I thought of that stupid hair and how much I had loved it, those long strands of keratin. The soft, sensual feel of it when the wind was blowing. The fragrance of it when freshly washed.
Goddess touching it with her breath before cutting it. Before killing me. Poor sucker me. All that lovin' gone bad. All that hair in a pool of blood.
She just sat there watching me.

"So why do you think she did it? To punish you?"
"You wouldn't understand. "

"Try me!"

"It was a gift. Not a punishment! A reward!"

"I see."

"No. Actually, you don't. You can't. You think it's ugly, don't you?"

"No, it suits you."

"Aha, so it *is* ugly?"

"No it is sexy, actually. It looks good on you."

She blushed. The she straightened her back, appalled by her own utterly unprofessional behaviour, and she continued in a kind, but formal, almost condescending tone of voice.

"I mean it suits you; you have an exquisitely shaped head and neck. It makes you look a bit like that rock star...what's-her-name...? Irish one... Big, huge sad deer eyes, like a scared defiant animal, like you."

She interrupted herself.

"Gosh... What *is* the matter with me? I am usually so... "

She cleared her throat.

"Anyway, have you spoken to ... Goddess ... lately?"

"What answer will render me a kiss?" I asked and let my elongated lizard tongue move to the top of my lip while sending her a hot glance.

"Is that a no?"

"You are the doctor, Doc. You tell me. The answer is at the tip of my tongue and I'm bilingual and ambivalent and dead, and probably talking to myself, anyway, so maybe it's a "*yes*" but I'm figuratively, literally, and physically open for suggestions from an expert. Try me!"

"So tell me, why are you here? Among us? The living? If you are dead?"

"Dead is in the eye of the beholder."

"A quite original way of looking at it."

"Depends on the perspective. Of the soul. Or, position, rather."

"Tell me, then. From the perspective of your soul!"

"It was a test."

"A test?"

"Are you into make-believe doctor?"

"Our goal is to make you well."

"I happen to know some positions we can try out that will save us both months of therapy."
She laughed.

"That is impossible. And you know that!"

"Well, here's the deal, Doc. I have to receive the love from a human being, a woman, in order to regain the love from my Goddess. To get my life back."

"It sounds a little like a fairytale. Did you read many fairytales as a child?"

"No. Didn't have to. I lived in one."

"A good one or a bad one?"

"A real one. I had a goddess for a godmother, remember? Just imagine me with my boundless imagination and her with her omnipotent powers... not to speak of her connections in high places! O, lá lá!"

"You are so funny, do you know that?"

"Actually it wasn't my intention. I was a minor but the law couldn't reach her, so to speak. Well, I guess it *is* funny after all."
Dr Zeus laughed again.
"I like your sense of humour. You are a romantic at heart, Sche-Hera Zade. Lovely name, by the way! Sounds familiar!"
She smiled, knowingly, presumably. Thinking she was smarter than I.

But at the end of the rainbow I could feel Goddess waiting, smiling, pleased with me and my sense of humour.

Dr Zeus was cute and couldn't hide it, probably because she wasn't fully aware of just how cute she was, the full extent of her cuteness so to speak, and the physical effect it had on me and my libido.
    She always walked in a determined way, like she was going somewhere, somewhere else, somewhere important, and somewhere where I wasn't sitting ogling her in my ugly clothes, with a pounding ache between my legs and in my heart.

She wore sophisticated 1000 dollar frame glasses to hide the occasional innocent childish sparkle in her big beautiful drown-me-slowly-blue eyes. She was highly ambitious and immensely successful in her profession, but her skin was starved for touch, a pain to listen to her skin it was, such scared and sad skin, really, - thin, artificially lubricated, too, in order not to break from lack of touch, just dissolve into thin air like dust, from failure to evoke love.

She glued her skin together with expensive artificial moisture.

Kept it together. In one piece.

With glue.

She hid her body like she hid her true self, like an obedient, sedated, domesticated animal behind expensive artificial skin grey wool business suits.

She was so afraid of life, my Darling Doc.

When she spoke she disguised her insecurities and real lack of knowledge behind big impressive words, as transparent, and impenetrable, and hard as the lenses of her glasses.

I actually told her this on our second therapy session. I told her I had had all her impressive psychology lingo word for breakfast a long time ago and discovered they were all soufflés made out of fake eggs.

She replied, lovely blonde head slightly tilted, amused, that she found the metaphor interesting, charming too, and quite intelligent, actually, comparing words to eggs!

That was when I first realised she had a great sense of humour, too, which she managed to hide the way she was hiding all signs of life,  so well she wasn't aware of it, herself.

I guess it was the way her lips moved when she tasted my words that turned me on and made me decide to tell her my secrets. To have her taste them, pronounce them, ingest them. Enter her. Impregnate her. Possess her.
(Well, to see how she liked it, basically.)

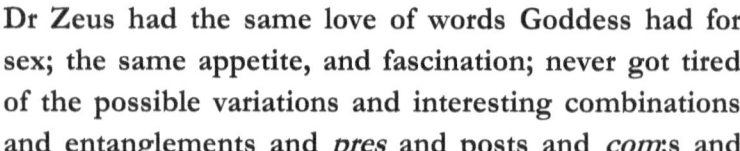

Dr Zeus had the same love of words Goddess had for sex; the same appetite, and fascination; never got tired of the possible variations and interesting combinations and entanglements and *pres* and posts and *com*:s and bi:s, and oxymoron and hyperbole and  metaphors.

So when I decided to tell her about my adventures with Goddess, I combined the two and I used the words she liked the most, the ones soaked in lust and brutality, curiosity and impatience, and with a naked itch so strong it is addictive.

So the next day, on our third session, I told her about one of Goddess's and my adventures.

I started out with the sweet little story of the nine muses and how we were introduced in a cloud of music on a bed of lust. How they held me softly and introduced me to my erogenous zones by playing me, licking me, singing me, drawing me.

"Nine of them, all licking you...? The voluptuous women, who were they?"

"Helpers, holders, holy hide-insiders."

"And you say you climaxed, for ... how long...?"

She sounded more impressed than anything.

"Five hours. Then Goddess got bored."

"You said she got bored easily?"

"Nah, five hours is a long time, even for a goddess."

"And, how did you feel?"

"Great, just great. Goddess introduced me to my libido and I got attached to it...."

"...And she licked me inside, while the curvaceous vanilla ladies spread my legs wide for her. And she let me decide who she would be. Sometimes, not always. And fucking was like music, the best sort, the sort that makes your blood sing. Rock music pounding in your blood, you being the music, dissolving into music ... Exactly like music but inside the body, playing you, everywhere, pounding inside the blood. Hard. Happy. Wet. Wanting. And horny like hell...."

"Can you elaborate?"

"Goddess took possession of a body, inhabited a body, any body, the body of a human, or an animal, a spirit, a ghost, anyone would do. Randomly. Whatever she felt like at the time. She liked to surprise me."

"Surprise you?"

"Like that time when I was sixteen, and ended up at a hospital with a broken rib a black eye and four long scars, (and not being a virgin any longer)."

"Are you sure that was her doing? According to the police report-..."

"Come-on! It was a test! You could say I passed. When I had recovered from the injuries we made fun of her little joke. Her collection grew during those months of healing."

"Her "*collection*"?"

"Of my tears."

"I see. And the five young men, the perpetrators, and the accident a week later. How did you feel about that?"

"Their bodies were never found. They were abducted by aliens. They will return any day now. Wiser. Kinder. And ... gay."

"Are you sure about that?"

"Yeah. Goddess planted the rumour about the accident. Her sense of humour. So can you imagine the look on people's faces when those guys will return just in time for dinner in a month or two? And gay on top of it!"

Dr Zeus contemplated this for a while. But she didn't smile.

I guess it's because she never had time for dinner, herself. She was very thin. Words was her drug of choice, not food. No real eggs for Dr Zeus.

On the fourth day I told her about the Mini Masqueraders in the Cave Castles and the Delights of Darkness.

"Those are fantasies. Delusions. We both know that."

"All words are pale reflections of reality. It comes with the territory. Whatever you prefer to call it we had better sex than anyone, especially you, Zeus-Anne, will ever have in a million years with your Mr Marathon Man. Plain Truth."

"Plain truth, huh? Tell me more about plain truth!"

"Plain truth is that you are wet, Dr. Zeus."
She avoided my glances.

"If you don't mind, I would prefer if you didn't speak to me like that. It's a sign of disrespect."

"The opposite, actually. You have no idea how much I truly respect you. That is why I bring you gifts." I smiled.

"*Gifts?*"

"You know exactly what I mean doctor. You prefer words to flowers, any day. Words will keep you company at night. Words will do things to you that flowers won't. Can't."

"No offence." I said.

("None taken." replied the single rose in the crystal vase on her desk.)

She blushed - and embarrassed and annoyed by her own utter lack of professionalism in front of me, a patient (!) - she continued to avoid my glance and wrote something down with the fat Montblanc fountain pen in her trembling hand.

Then finally she managed to get a grip on herself and gave me a shy smile and laughed a little while she threw some glances at the tiny tape recorder on her desk.

"You will be the ruin of me; you do know that, don't you?" She said almost inaudibly, as if she was talking to herself, still smiling, cheek flushed.

Then she looked up and saw me smiling.

"*Holy shit! You heard that!*"

I laughed at her choice of words, and her embarrassment, and finally she relaxed a little.

She wasn't used to laughing, but once she had started she couldn't stop, delighted in the happy feeling inside her tummy.

"You must know that it is physiologically impossible to climax for that long." she said.

"Unfortunately!" she added with a faint smile.

I returned the smile.

"Well let's put it this way. I am so glad I didn't know at the time."

Dr Zeus laughed again.

"Excellent point."

"And I guess the experience didn't do me any real harm, either." I added.

"I don't know about that, it might have spoiled you for ordinary humans." she joked.

"No. On the contrary, I am the best lover you will ever find, Zeus-Anne, because I love—"

"Let's be serious for a moment, shall we." she interrupted me, suddenly annoyed about her own appalling lack of professionalism whenever she was anywhere near me.

———⟶

She still didn't believe in the truth so I gave her the censored version, the pathetic little fifteen orgasm version, which was so hot she had to fiddle with some object on her desk now and then, and fan herself with the pamphlet not to burst.

There was a glow to her that intensified when I recapitulated my adventures with Goddess.

Whenever we were alone in her office her aura was glowing and sparkling.

It was magic.

Pure magic and nothing else.

What else is there?

My words and my eyes held her captive in a bubble of magic.

My words were taking liberties with her skin and her nerves, touching her like tiny fingers, teasing her.

My words made her squeeze her thighs together and ache for my real fingers.

She didn't tell me this, only played with her pen or readjusted her glasses and muttered *"interesting, very interesting"*, and said *"uhum is that so,"* nod, while pretending to write things down with her trembling hand while glancing at my fingers and clearing her throat.

Around me she could no longer move outside our multicoloured cage of magic. Not that she wanted to.
She liked it when I kept her trapped inside, teasing her with my words while my eyes were kissing her.
Electricity.
Energy.
Our libidos mingled, like a party of two, in a rite of seduction in the air between us.
Day and night held hands in our dance of magic.
She could feel it but pretended not to.
I liked her coyness.
I knew how she would taste even before I had touched her.
Even before I had tasted her.
I watched her suffer because I knew everything about her.
She wanted me to kill her tenderly, so she could begin living.

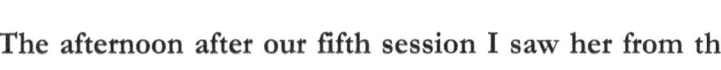

The afternoon after our fifth session I saw her from the window of my cell, talking to her husband.

Too polite to listen, I only listened to the interesting parts, which were just a bag of baloney, anyway; shitty, smug, bloated, farty words, no poetry, no ambiguity, no allusions, no kindness, or sincerity, anyway; not worth the effort, might as well have licked the pukey grey walls of my cell instead.

Her body language told me that she didn't love him. Actually she didn't even like him. I wouldn't go as far as to say she despised him, only notice that she shuddered as if touched by a rotting corpse when he touched her arm. Then again she was a physician, and a real professional at that, and being an expert, she could hide her repulsion of human kind, of male kind, or dead kind, for that matter, from the world. But she couldn't hide her repulsion of that man from me - not from me.

I could tell they had had an argument and she shouted something to him with tears in her eyes, trembling hands, and I could see the mean, cruel streak in his eyes when he replied something, with a sarcastic, superior grin on his thin lips, and suddenly I knew what he did to her when nobody was around to protect her.

I knew, being a physician himself, he was too smart, too sophisticated, to leave any marks or bruises on her delicate body.

Only her beautiful, sensitive soul was damaged and severely so, irreparably so.

Such cruelty mustn't, shouldn't, couldn't pass unnoticed, and in just a few minutes the ambulance arrived. And there he lay, on the ground, not technically dead, but corrected, rather.

Dr Zeus turned around with her hand before her mouth and I blew her a kiss from my window. I smiled back at her, and laughed a little, because at that moment she looked absolutely adorable, just like a little girl.

"I love you." I murmured from my window. "I'll do anything for you. For as long as it takes. Tell you any story you like, kill anyone you hate. You name it, Doc."

I could tell she was surprised and slightly puzzled. Far more surprised than upset, actually, which pleased me immensely. *"That's my girl! Getting stronger by the minute!"*


Until then she had never really believed in my recollections of my affair with Goddess.

Rationality was her religion of choice, and it had made her unhappy, as is of course the purpose of all organized religions, science included.

At that moment she was even more beautiful than Goddess; at those rare moments Goddess had allowed me to look at her through a mirror.

———→

The next day she was silent and looked very sad. She tried to smile but failed.

"Please, tell me a story, any story!" she said. "You promised to tell me about the *blowkite balloonie dykes*."

"How about your delusions? I know everything about you, Zeus. Why you are so sad. Why you are having second thoughts about your choices in life, and why you think you can help others when you aren't able to solve any of your own problems, and why you didn't cry when your mother died, and why you can't remember her ever telling you she loved you, or once tell you that she was proud of you..."

Dr Zeus was staring at me.

"... and why you are sad because Dr Morgan and Dr Smith are publically opposing your research ... and why you married a verbally and physically abusive man, when you always preferred women."

She bit her lip hard and I could she was crying, silently. She was trembling, and she didn't mind me seeing it.

"Yes he is such a bastard.... But you took care of that... didn't you?"

I rose and came up from behind. I approached her big mahogany desk and she didn't notice, enwrapped in her own thoughts.

I gently moved her hair from her neck and kissed her lightly. She didn't protest.

"You can t possibly think I had anything to do with it?" I said.

She sighed.

"I just don't know what to think anymore. Such a strange coincidence. Marcus is the fittest person I know. He ran the big five last year. You know the five biggest marathons in the world. He never had any incidents of heart failures before, ever... a health freak ... control freak..."

I caressed her face gently.

"Well there is a first for everything, isn't there, Zeus-Anne?"

My hand slid slowly down inside her blouse and at first she didn't seem to notice. My words had taken her by surprise and she was trying hard to come up with a rational explanation as to how it was possible that I could know her most intimate secrets, things she didn't even dare to confide to her Diary.

Then she noticed my hand and what it was doing and she bend her head back a little, sighed and relaxed, as my hand moved down inside her white lace bra with embroidered pink mini roses on it. Her nipple was hard.

She couldn't hold back a moan.

"Maybe you shouldn't..." she whispered. "Really this is not... appropriate."

"It is the only appropriate thing to do. All things considered. You know that, Doc."

So I whispered into her ear some of the things I must do to her.

Her aura was lovelier than ever before, Aurora Borealis eat your heart out.

I knew I would be cruel if I didn't fuck her.

My teeth played with her earlobe for a while and I noticed she had started to breathe a little faster.

"You know ... your stories-...." She sighed.

"I know, you record them and listen to them at home, alone at night, I know...over and over again... and they grow on you, don't they, and make you feel things and realize things..."

"Fairy tales, yes...and still... "I am a physician, married to a physician, and I never knew there were so many erogenous zones on the female body..."

"Fascinating, isn't it? Truth and truth?"

We both smiled as her eyes lit up in pure anticipation of what life, and I, might offer, if she only let us.

She asked:

"Do you think you will ever get over ... her ... and love anyone else...someone less talented?"

"The question is: will she let me? Maybe she will disguise herself as me, and fuck you? Just to fuck you up sexually and mentally. To spoil you for me. Her sense of humour can be hard to understand if you are not used to it."

"I want you, just you, the real stuff. The real thing. The really, really bad you, and the really, really good you. Go on - touch me now! Show me who you are! Don't use any word this time. Just use your hands, your fingers, your mouth..."

I kissed her and moved my hand down inside her lace panties and let it play a little with her soft folds and clit. She was wet and soft and lovely. I hadn't expected her to be this excited. She was on the verge of coming. I was on the verge of dying, too.

She was starving.

Starving for kindness, closeness, starving for touch, starving for sex, starving for tenderness.

She wanted me to kill her slowly, tenderly, so she could begin living.

Over and over again.

She wanted me to hold her in my arms. Caress her hair. Rock her gently. Whisper tender things into her ears. Sing to her. Over and over again.

Cherish her first breath of life. Over and over again.

Kiss her good morning. Over and over again.

Watch the good morning sparkle in her eyes. Watch the flush on her cheeks when our eyes meet over breakfast coffee.

Watch her devour food, as sensually as famished, as she devoured me, licking her fingers afterwards, tasting life. Delighted.

Eons of loneliness evaporated from my hands in tiny clouds. Essence of unhappiness – gone.

Her starving skin drank the love from my hands.

The softness of her skin surprised me. How much it needed the touch of my hands in order to survive.

We were on the floor. My fingers deep inside of her. Kissing. Fucking. Making love. Like animals and divine creatures.

"Tell me you are well. Please... do it *now*!"

"I can't do that; if I do I won't be able to see you everyday..."

"You are no sicker than I am, and no sadder, either, you just got it all in one blow, past present and future, all of it in one blow, and now you take refuge in your fantasy about a Goddess... confused and sad...that's all... tell me... teach me... touch me... more.."

She was crying.

The love in my touch made her cry.

Nobody had ever touched her like that before. Nobody had ever loved her like I do. Nobody had ever loved her. Before I did.

Her tears made me smile.

They were mine.

I collected them.

"You can come live with me. You know you can, Sche-Hera." She said.

"Can I?"

"There's   nothing wrong with you. Nothing. Life is brutal to all of us. Either we survive, or we don't. And we each survive in our own way. Nothing's wrong with you that isn't wrong with me. Come live with me. Be free with me."

"Can I?"

"On one condition only...you must tell me a story ...every night... for thousand and one nights...and then...we...we ... will live happily ever after."

And so I did.

Every night I tell her a new story. Then we make it happen.
And yes, we live happily. Why on earth shouldn't we?
Goddess makes sure of that.

### *The End*

PS. Any similarity to any living, dead or semi-dead mortal or Goddess is purely coincidental and all is fiction and nobody is truly alive, anyway. Ask any Goddess.

# "One Way Ticket to Always"

I watched her as she got off the bus and looked around the Bus Terminal.

I let her look. Look for me in the face of everyone.

Nothing is as sweet as hope.

Nothing more cruel.

I watched her from a distance, watched her taste it, with all her senses.

*"How do you define a person?*
*The only person that ever was? For you?*
*Always?*
*How do you speak to her?*
*After an eternity of hope without hope?*
*How do you look at her without falling apart inside?"*

My heart was beating so hard that I found it hard to breathe.

Then she saw me, standing there, watching her.

She looked genuinely surprised, as if deep down inside she refused to believe I'd be there; that I had simply forgotten everything about her and her phone-call the week before. She blushed and avoided my glance.

"So you came...!"

"Yes, of course. Why? Didn't you think I would?"

"I hoped so."

Her voice was almost inaudible.

"But-..." she added.

"What?"

"Oh, n-nothing."

We remained standing there, for a short moment, somehow drained of energy and in loss of words.

Some mornings when I happened to meet my own gaze in the bathroom mirror I was struck by the infinite sadness in my eyes; shocked by the pain my mind tried to hide from me, but was there, in the windows of my soul. Now I recognized the same sadness in Sindri's eyes.

"You know ...things aren't always what they appear to be..." she said.

I felt a lump in my throat and couldn't reply.

"Don't hate me! Please!" She continued, almost whispering. "Promise!"

I avoided her glance, her words. I cleared my throat and said:

"You must be very tired. Long trip!"

"Yes. I guess I am."

And she laughed a nervous, joyless laugh.

We remained silent in the taxi, as if there was an understanding between us not to speak in front of a witness. During the whole ride we were observing each other, with all our senses except our eyes.

I opened the door to my condominium. Sandra put down her leather suitcases and looked around the apartment. The sun played on the furniture and plants. Her eyes widened at the sight of my oil paintings, sketches and framed photographs, the heaps of books and magazines on the floor and bookshelves, and for a brief second she looked as I remembered her, the first time I ever saw her; glowing. She loved art and all its expressions with a passion she couldn't hide and now her entire being lit up for a second, as if for the first time in months her suffocating soul had managed to get a breath of pure oxygen.

Life, and sparks of her passion; her infatuation with art, and, with it, a hunger for life; returned to her ocean blue eyes for a brief second.

"Oh, I like it! It´s so nice!" she exclaimed. "Oh, I could-..."
She stopped herself.
"You could... what?"
"I could... visit you... sometimes... I mean, if you would invite me..."
"Sure! Why not? Next time, I'll invite you, ok? This time you invited yourself, remember?"
The words didn't come out as cheerfully as I intended and she immediately responded:
"This was Billy's idea. Not mine."
Her voice was soft but defensive; if it hadn't been for Billy she might not be here at all. And I replied, too quickly, too surly:
"Good old Billy sure knows how to get things done!"
Her eyes widened in horror, but it was too late. The words had left my mouth.
She opened her handbag and handed me an envelope.
"He wanted you to have this."
Her hand was trembling and she blushed.
"Thanks." I said. "I'll read it later. Promise!"
"He insisted that I'd be there when you read it."
"I see."
"He said it was written in your childhood secret language and that nobody but you would get anything out of it."

"Still, you could have just mailed it to me? Quite a trip just to deliver a letter!"

"He wanted you to know things. It was very important for him. It is important for me, too."

"Yes. And whatever Billy wants, Billy always gets. Right?"

Her eyes started to fill up with tears and she avoided my glances.

"Excuse me, where is the bathroom, please?"

"Over there, next to the atelier."

She closed the bathroom door I behind her. Through the noise of the running water inside, I could hear her throwing up.

I cursed my own stupid, inconsiderate comments and lack of restraint.

Sindri was so pale when she returned from the bathroom that I was afraid she would faint. But the only thing I could think of saying was:

"You must be hungry?"

"Hungry...?"

She had to think for a minute; trying to recall the concept of hunger and its relevance to her body.

I suggested that she rest for a while in the sofa while I prepared a light meal for us. I opened a bottle of wine. Now and then I threw a glance at her. She seemed lost somehow, curled up in my big comfortable couch, hugging a pillow like a small, obedient child; while trying to remember to act her age, and to behave, while not knowing how to trust reality.

"No wine, please!"
She covered the wine glass with her thin hand, and turned away.

"No?"

"Not good for me right now. I am-... tired..."

"It's ok; I don't want you to fall asleep on me. Not quite yet!" I joked.

We sat down at the dining room table.
She closed her eyes while she tasted the grilled salmon and vegetables. My cooking skills pleased her, and the delicious sensations made her relax. After a few bites she asked, eyes still closed, savoring the world of subtle pleasures:

"Raven; do you remember that day on the beach?"

"Yes."

"You, me, Billy, and your mom. The sea; so calm, and gentle that day. The sand, so soft and warm, like tingling skin. The sun ... ah, the sun...so loving, to all creatures."

She smiled, enwrapped in the memories, and spoke very fast now, in little gusts; hanging on to the sweet emotion.

"Oh, Raven! Raven; Do you remember that little girl who threw her ball at Billy? So tiny! And so cute with her tiny pony tail and little sneakers, and Dolores, how she got all teary-eyed, remember, when she observed Billy with the little girl?"

"Yes. Mom was happy that day. The two of you really made her happy."

My voice was dry.

"You know; I never understood why he wanted to be with me. Billy could have had anyone."

*"He did."* I thought. *"He had them all. When you were not around."*

"Why me?"

"Don't they have mirrors where you come from?"

"What do you mean?"

She wasn't being cute, or fishing for compliments. She was simply too sad, and too exhausted to understand my hint.

"Your smile...Well I maybe you don't know, but your smile..."

I turned away.

*"Your smile makes me believe there is a God."* I thought.

I cleared my throat and said, in a light tone of voice, studying the label of the wine bottle.

"Come-on, Sindri; you have such a wonderful smile. You must know that."

"I ...must? No. No. I mean...I *do*...? No, no. I mean, thank you!"

She turned red. Then she quickly escaped the strange atmosphere between us, by returning to the memories of the day at the beach.

"Imagine, how you went away to buy ice cream for all of us all, for the little girl, too. Oh, that strawberry ice cream cone, the best I have ever tasted, my favorite flavor, how did you know...?. You were gone for so long, while Billy and I and Dolores were just relaxing in the

sun, Billy made up goofy stories about his friends, made
your mom laugh so hard she had to beg him to stop."
She smiled, and then she frowned:

"You had to walk far, to get those ice cream cones,
didn't you?"

"No big deal; I just wanted to get the best there was,
for you."

"Yes, you always wanted what was best for us, didn't
you?" She said, unable to hide a serious note in her
voice.

"It did take a while, I guess." I said. "To get that ice
cream, I mean."

"It did. You were gone for a long time."
She looked sad again, like she had too much weight on
her mind.

"I know you never wanted to me to be with your
brother. But you were always so polite about it."
I didn't reply. What could I say? That the sight of Billy
and her together was more than I could stand, but not
for the reason she believed?

We sat in the sofa, Billy saturating the space between us
with his invisible presence, making it hard to speak, to
breathe, even.

Suddenly Sindri started to cry, her entire body shook,
and the more she tried to hold back her violent
emotions, the more she cried. She covered her face in
her hands.

I moved closer and put my arms gently around her.

"*Sorry. Sorry. Sorry.*" She sobbed.

"Come-on, come-on, now..."

"You know ... I always wanted you to like me. And now ... it's too late..."

"I always ... liked you."

"Oh no. You were always very kind, but the way you looked at us was ...repulsed. Sort of."

"You really are being too emotional. Of course I liked you. Come-on! You were married to my brother! "

"Wrong reason! Wrong, wrong, wrong reason!"
The sudden spark of anger, drowned in a wave of sadness mixed with guilt in her big ocean blue eyes.
And I thought:
"*But how can I tell you the real reason? That I love you and have loved you from the moment I first saw you?*"

"I'm sorry; I don't know why I behave like this. I sound like a five-year-old..."

"You have been through a lot." I said.

"Yes, things have been pretty rough lately. First Billy ... and then those weird phone calls in the middle of the night. Strangers staring. They all blame me for it... All of them....."

"Nobody blames you ..."

"But they do. You, too! I always mess up everything... Don't I?"
I smiled.

"Yes, actually you do mess up things. A little."
"*You messed me up.*" I thought. "*You really did. Completely.*"

"Do you know what's in the letter?" I asked.

"He said it was important for him, for us all, that you knew the truth about something."
She was silent for a while.

"At the time I didn´t really know what he meant ... he just mentioned that he wanted a one way ticket ...fed up with everything, with the city, his crowd. Me. That sort of thing. I never thought he intended to-..."

"Was he depressed?"

"He must have been. Why else...? We... we ...did argue a lot. He said I was too jealous. He wanted... out..."

I opened the sealed envelope.

The letter was in Billy's handwriting. It took me a few minutes to remember the secret language we had developed during those days in hell in our childhood.

I could feel her eyes resting on me when I read the letter.

*"Raven,*
*I want you to have the money. You saved my life that time. You never talked about it. So take the money.*
*I will tell them I blew it in Vegas.*
*They will make it look like suicide. I can't escape them.*
*They are everywhere.*
*I won't come back and haunt you.*
*I don't believe in that stuff. But never say never.*
*Reunions can be fun!*
*Ha ha ha! Boo! See you in Hell, Sis.*
*Forgot.*
*You are not going in that direction!*
*See you in Nirvana!*

*Keep an eye on Sindri for me.*
*PS. Money is in the tree. You know which one.*
*Billy Your Big Bro."*

I blew my nose.
"I had no idea..." I said. "No idea whatsoever..."
"Nobody did."
"What can I say? You never...?"
"No. I was hospitalized for a few days."
"*Hospitalized?*" I thought.
"Sad?"
"Sad? Well, yes. That, too, I guess." She said.
"Why didn't you leave him?"
"Too dangerous."
"Can I sleep with you tonight? You know I was the one who found him... And at night ... when I close my eyes I can still see ... him... and ... all the blood....!"

I knew that having her sleeping next to me it would be a sublime form of sensual torture and I didn't know how I would be able to endure it. But my sufferings were of a different magnitude than hers, and I couldn't imagine the horrors that she had to deal with every night when her memories returned to haunt her.
"Do you want to take a bath, first?" I asked.
"Yes. Yes please."
I joined her in the bathroom and helped her get a towel and poured bath oil into the tub and checked the temperature of the water, and did a million little things while she got undressed.

After all these months I couldn't deny myself the innocent pleasure of watching her naked body. And even though she was a bit shy, she was too polite to ask me to leave.

She removed her indigo blue cashmere polo, slowly, sensually, like a stripper.

At first I couldn't understand why. Was she trying to seduce me? My body was convinced she was, and responded immediately, and in a second I was so turned on that my legs got faint.

Then I saw the scar.

There was a long fresh scar on her back and on the upper part of her right arm. It looked obscene on her soft vulnerable skin. Like a hideous tattoo.

"My god! What happened to your back? Your arm?" I yelled.

"But Raven- ...you just read the letter...?"

"Yes?"

"So you *know!*"

It took a few seconds for the pieces to fit together.

"Oh, my god...oh my god...oh my god..."


And now it was my turn to hide my face in my hands.

I had always known that my brother was violent and hot tempered and I had often heard him express harsh opinions about women, but I had never expected him to beat up his girlfriends. It didn't make any sense to me that he would be capable of doing such a horrible thing to a woman knowing how much he worshipped our mother.

My tears made her forget her shyness and when Sindri turned around I realized that she must be the most beautiful and desirable thing on earth; so close but yet so unattainable, that she might as well have been a random reflection from a parallel galaxy.

My body began to tremble from the mix of violent emotions that emerged.

"You were always so sensitive." She said.

"Was I?" I said and blew my nose.

"Yes. Very. So very different from Billy." she said, and she couldn't hide the tenderness in her voice.

She borrowed an oversized t-shirt and we went to bed. I was careful to turn off the lights and only leave a few candles burning, hoping I would be able to hide my feelings better in the dark.

We crawled under the cover, her back against my chest, the two of us enwrapped in a lovely fragrance of lavender from the fresh sheets and the scents from her own body.

She pressed herself against me, strands of her soft hair tickling my nose.

"Hold, me please." She said. "I really, really need it."

Our bodies close, I listened to her heart. It was the heart of a scared animal. Her nipples teasing me when my arms brushed against them; her body so soft; so strong.... I swam in the feeling, dizzy...

"Why are you smiling?" she asked after a while.

"How can you tell I am smiling? Do you have eyes in your neck?"

"Dunno. Your body tells me so. And your voice."

"But I haven't said anything ..."

"I guess it's an echo of something you will say, then, in the future...A time warp, as you used to say, science-fiction-geek you..."

She giggled and moved her feet and I gave out a little scream.

"My feet are cold." She said. "Sorry. Must be the time warp factor. Are you smiling yet, Raven?"

I was. My heart was smiling. My entire body was smiling, melting, swimming in sensations.

"Let me warm those poor little feet." I said. "I happen to be a foot-warming expert. The best in town. Or in bed."

I gave her tiniest toe a tiny peck.

When I looked up at her, her eyes were filled with tears again.

"You are so kind to me. How come? How can you be?"

Something in my eyes, or my breathing, or in the way I kissed her precious little toe, made her realize the truth.

I was so excited it hurt.

"Do you like ... women ...?" she asked.

"I like you." I said. "Only you."

"Did you just ... realize it? I mean... right now?"

I couldn't help laughing. There was innocence to her that was so genuine, that not even Billy, the poster-boy of cynicism, had been able to ruin it.

"Are you attracted to me, Raven?" she whispered.

"Please, please, please, don't ask me that...!"

"But I never thought...The idea never occurred..."

"What?"

"But you had a boyfriend!"

"So? Who doesn't these days?"

She didn't laugh.

"But..."

"Mom always gave me those accusing *"When is it my turn to have a grandchild?"*-looks. The least I could do for her was to get a boyfriend. One she could brag about. Joaquin was there and he was and remains my best friend."

She caressed my cheek.

"I like you too, you know." She said. "I fantasized a lot about you. Wild and silly fantasies of how you would come and save me. And how you would look at me the way you looked at your dog."

I laughed.

"That didn't sound so good."

"With that look in your eyes. Recognition.

"Nothing else? Just ... recognition?"

She laughed.

"Yes. Recognition."

I smiled but didn't reply, so she continued.

"I observed you when you didn't know it. You were always on your guard, so polite and distant, but with your little dog you could relax. You became all soft and so different. You looked so young somehow. So happy. You whispered little things to that little dog. Oh, how I wished I had been that little dog... I envied her. I would have given anything to have you look at me the way you looked at that little dog."

I smiled.

"Your dog didn't like me."

"Varg, her name was Varg. I adopted Varg from an animal shelter. She didn't trust anyone but me. My little Varg had suffered a lot of abuse in her short life ..."

I looked at her and she was crying again.

"Poor little creature. I have suffered abuse, too, you know!" she cried. "I know I sound pathetic... Please don't laugh..."

"How could I? You are so horribly, horribly depressed, my love." I said.

I kissed her forehead.

"Why did you call me that?"

"Call you what? Depressed?"

"*My love?*"

"Why? Because you are. I have loved you from the moment I first laid my eyes on you. "

"You have?"

I could feel her body relax, and all the tension leave, like a bad spirit taking its leave. She took my hand and started to play with it, the way a small child plays with your hand, bending my fingers, straightening them, as she spoke, getting familiar with my hand.

"I'm so glad he told you about what he did to me." She said. "You see, Raven; he always blamed me for his anger. Always. And I always did too."

"Don't think about that now." I said. "Don't blame yourself. We have insanity running in our family..."

"Oh no!"

"Something horrible happened to us when we were children, and Billy never got over it. I guess that could explain some of his rage."

♻

"I always wondered what it would be like to kiss you." She smiled.

"You did? Really?"

"Yes, there comes softness over you when you don't know you are observed. I imagined your hands over me, my breasts, my ..."

"You mean, your little..."

I let my hand slowly move down her body, over the little bulge of a tummy, rest between her legs and touch her lightly. There.

She trembled, and moaned.

"Yes...Just like that."

She moaned and started to move her hips involuntary.

"Now you must kiss me!" she whispered in a throaty voice.

So I kissed her. Our tongues played slowly. I could have kissed her forever. It was a tender kiss but still the most exciting thing I had ever experienced.

"Have you ever... you know...with a woman?" she asked.

"Yes."

"Did you like it?"

"We just ... fucked."

"And. ...did you like the just fucking?"

She tasted the word and liked the effect it had on her body. (So did I.)

"Yes, believe it or not; the less I liked the women the more I liked the fucking. I guess I tried to fuck myself to death, and sometimes it was divine. Fuck-Heaven. While it lasted. Afterwards- . Well, I just wanted to die. Do you think I am disgusting?"

"No, but you might not like fucking me. Or – worse - if you like fucking me I will know that you don't like me."

I couldn't help laughing.

She joined me.

"You and I will make love."

"Fucking is fine with me." She said. "For starters. I really want you to like me."

She made a pause.

"Me and ...."

"You and...?"

She took my hand and placed it on her tummy.

"Me and our baby."

There is a taste to the hungry skin that only the hungry hand can read; A kinship and a bond that can't be broken. I read it as she sung it to me. I was happy.

Always.

*The End*

~

# "Date night, right?"

~

Josie and I were sitting in a room packed with women. The chairs were uncomfortable but Josie didn't care. I did. I was bored stiff. We were anticipating the arrival of a woman, but not just any woman; we were waiting for Mayona Ness, the famous writer of *"Date night – date right, a girl's perfect manual for the perfect date."*

One of us was definitely looking forward to the arrival of the famous writer and it wasn't me.

But a deal is a deal. Josie had promised to come with me to the animal shelter the next day –because I was hoping that she would be so charmed by Mini, Tiny, Boogie, Lim, and old Sarah, that she would help me find homes for them-, and I had promised to come with her to the

old book store where the reading would take place -
because Josie was hoping I would be so inspired and
enlightened by the reading that it would help me get a
date, -which Josie felt I needed as much as the dogs
needed new homes.    Josie   grabbed   my   arm   rather
violently. Mayona Ness was entering the room!
   "*Oh look-look-look! There she is! Look at her!*"

I did, and so did everybody else. Mayona Ness was
dressed in a tight purple dress and wore dangerously
high heel emerald shoes. A long delicate shawl that
seem to weigh nothing and reflect all colors imaginable
floated like a fiery cloud around her slim body. She wore
her strawberry blonde hair in a lose bun.
   It was impossible to tell how old she was, only that
the warmth from her being was touching my being like
the rays from a newborn day. I think even the neglected
old dusty books on the shelves felt a jolt of electricity.
   Josie, who   subscribed   to   at   least   five   fashion
magazines, was star struck.
   "Look at her! Her hair! Her skin! Her boobs! Her
legs! Those shoes! That dress! She is absolutely
*gorgeous*. It's a *miracle* she is still single!"
   "I would be single, too, if I looked like her!"
   "You are single, Wyn. Remember!?"
   "Yes. That's why we have nothing in common."
Unfortunately my clever remark didn't silence Josie for
more than two seconds, - and not the ten minutes I had
hoped for. She gave me a quick glance with her big
brown eyes:

"No need to look so sad, honey-pie! You know Josie only wants what's best for you."

"And what's that? Oh no! Please don't tell!"

"*Love*! I want you to stare out in space with a silly smile on your face."

*"Some people are not meant for love. It is just that simple."* I thought.

Over at the podium the star was arranging her books and notes, touching the microphone on the big desk, assisted by a doting employee who ran back and forth bringing things; a bottle of mineral water and a box of napkins, and a bouquet of blue irises, and as a final touch, a group of assorted scented block candles to create an ambience of intimacy.

"You'd better listen carefully now!" whispered Josie. "It's been two years now since the divorce! Two years! And not a single date!"

"So?"

"No fun! No sex! No man in your life."

*"Nor will there ever be again."* I thought. *"But I can't tell you why. You are my best friend, Josie! What if I told you and you would turn all uncomfortable and tense around me?!"*

∿

Mayona Ness grabbed the microphone and her eyes swept around the room:

"*Toot, toot*! Is everybody comfortable out there? Just checking!"
At least seventy star struck faces were beaming back at her; watching her intently; expecting miracles from her soft peach colored mouth and warm, sensual voice.

"Not too comfortable, I hope? I intend to be merciless tonight, because suffering is part of a good date, part of the overall build up, the anticipation, and I want you to be ready. So suffer babes, suffer! You will thank me later! Promise!"

Soft ripples of laughter and squeaking of chairs from the audience. The high volt energy mixed with anticipation and strong scents reminded me of the animal shelter and my four-legged friends. So far so good.

"Hi, lovely ladies! My name is Mayona Ness! And, yes, that really is my name, long story, do not ask, and I repeat: Do not ask, because the first person laughing at my name I will personally kick out of this lovely room with my lovely seven hundred dollar shoes! And I mean it!"
There was an uncomfortable buzz in the room and squeaking of chairs.

"Just kidding! Now I have got your attention and that is what it is all about!"
Relieved giggles and laughter in the room.

"Excuse me, what is "*what it is all*" about?" asked one woman in the audience.

"Getting the attention! Making an impression! Make them notice you. The kick in the soft spot; in the "*got-to-have-her-spot!*"

"Why are you smiling?" whispered Josie. "Having an aha-moment already?"

"Yes! Remember when Ziggy got adopted, Josie? How she got the attention of everybody -...."
Josie put her finger to her mouth and hushed:
"Later, ok?"


Something about the way Mayona Ness was leaning on the desk and held her book in her hand reminded me of Hamlet and the skull and a monologue about being or not being...*something*... being *what* ...?
I couldn't remember but I decided against asking Josie.


"For those of you who haven't read my book or heard of me: A long time ago I shared some fool proof dating advice with my girlfriends. Someone suggested I'd share my secrets with the rest of womankind. I firmly believe in sharing good things and moments. So here we are ladies, sharing this moment!"

"I like the cover a lot!" said a woman in the audience.

"Fascinating. So does my publisher. That makes two of you. What do you like about it? The 2D- feel? Up and down and go for it?"

"I don't know but it's sexy, isn't it? I mean the woman looks kind of naked, doesn't she? And the man doesn't."

"I believe they are both wearing something. But it's definitely not Armani, or Chanel or Vera Wang. They probably borrowed some leftovers from Project Runaway first Season Grocery Store Assignment, but unfortunately I can't ask the cover artist because she is presently hiding in an Ashram in India. "

She bit her lip in order not to laugh at her own joke. Some of the women in the room looked slightly uncomfortable. I was the only one laughing, apart from Mayona Ness herself, and perhaps I was a bit too loud.

Mayona Ness looked up and looked around the room. And when her eyes landed on me she looked at me, really, really looked at me, without restraint; the way a young child or young animal absorbs you with their eyes without blinking, in a perfectly innocent way; only that Mayona Ness's way of looking at me was the opposite of innocent, but perfect, if that makes sense, which it didn't, of course, to anyone but me.

And then she smiled with her eyes, and touched the tip of her high heel shoe with two fingers. And whistled. It looked very feminine and provocative and sexy somehow.

At least to me it did.

The rest of the women in the audience looked confused.

I promised myself that one of these days I was going to get shoes like hers and practice charisma.

"Why are you blushing, Donwenna?" asked Josie.
"Oh… well…You know me and shoes."

"No I don't know about you and shoes! You are so full of secrets."

"Me? *Secrets*? Come-on!"

I started to laugh again.

Imagine! I had developed a fetishism for shoes in just fifteen minutes. Amazing! Just like my four-legged friends at the animal shelter.

When I saw Mayona Ness standing there, radiating human warmth and joy, I suddenly realized how lonely I was. And for once it had nothing to do with the neglected animals at the shelter, but with myself and my own neglected heart.

Mayona Ness was telling us about the art of listening and paying attention to what was *not* said, which according to her was the most important part of the conversation, and apparently the silent part, the bull shit part of her talk, didn't make any sense to anyone but me.

When she mentioned the words "alpha male" and "politics" and "lingerie" in the same sentence, I started to laugh so hard I almost fell to the floor. I just couldn't stop myself. Maybe I was tired? Tired and sad always made me laugh and cry simultaneously; especially when someone cracked jokes that weren't intended to be jokes but truths; especially when that someone was someone lovely beyond words and beyond dreams, beyond this life and beyond any death.

The women sitting next to me gave me strange looks.

Josie whispered: "You seem amused? So what do you think of her? Any good advice so far?"

I whispered back:

"She is wonderful, simply wonderful, so self-confident, and so beautiful. More than beautiful. Radiant. She has bucket of charisma. No, not just buckets, oceans, no, not just oceans, universes, universa? Univ---"

Josie sighed, patiently.

"Yes, yes, yes; I get it - no need to elaborate...."

I whispered: "...- and so, so, so *funny*..."

Josie was watching me with an expression I couldn't make out. Very observant, suspicious almost, a tiny wrinkle on her forehead, and she whispered:

"Yes. But she is a bit full of herself, too, don't you think; a bit cocky, and she has those little weird ticks and strange incomprehensible jokes, just like you. It might scare men off, you know."

*"Perfect!"* I thought. *"Who knows, I might buy the book after all!"*

I enjoyed everything Mayona Ness said but more than anything the way she said it, and especially the way she looked when she said it, but more than anything I enjoyed the way she made me feel when she said it, looking the way she did, when she said it, so when the reading was over, I decided to buy the book and to have it signed and to read from it to Zoë, Gaia, Gandhi, my soul mate dogs.

It made them relax when I read to them, and especially when I told them to listen carefully and pay attention to details. Who knows? Maybe they would get lucky?

*ᴧ*

Josie and I joined the long line of women in front of the desk where Mayona Ness was sitting signing her books. When it was our turn she looked up at us and gave us a broad smile.

"Hi there! And *you*...!"

She pointed to me with her lovely index finger:

"...you are the one who laughed at ALL my jokes! Appreciate it!"

She opened the book and lifted her fat Montblanc fountain pen and when she looked at me her gaze was so intense I felt weak in my knees. Lucky for me I wore sneakers and was leaning on the desk with both my hands to disguise how much they were trembling.

"What's your name, funny lady?"

"Dwynwen; oh, just write "*Hello ... Wen...*" I said.

She smiled and lifted the pen and wrote, pronouncing each word carefully:

"Hello.... *When?* .... Dwynwen."

She looked up from the book and gave me a quick glance:

"... Mayona Ness...Want some Mayona Ness with that, Dwynwen?"

"Yes, please!"

"On top or under?"

Blushing like a young girl I grabbed the book with both my hands because they were trebling so much that I was afraid I would drop the book.

"So impatient! She can't wait to get back to the dogs!" said Josie and handed over her own copy and gave me a reassuring little pat on the shoulder.

"Don't say that! They are not all that bad." said Mayona Ness. "Some men are really sweet little things."

"She works at an animal shelter!" said Josie.

"Whoops!" said Mayona Ness. "Hope my publisher didn't hear that!"
She pretended to look around the room and under the desk.

When I opened my backpack, to put my signed copy inside, the backpack slipped out of my hand and at least twenty five photocopied pictures of my four legged friends fell on a pile on the floor. Maybe it was a sign from my subconscious guide to get back? Return to my flock?

"I really need to get on my back, to get back, get homes... I mean ...For them... Get home...They need me to get home...  homes for them!" I said and turned red again.
*"Shit!"* I felt so stupid.

Both Mayona Ness and Josie gave me inquisitive looks.

I just wanted to get back to my dogs. They didn't care if I behaved odd around people. They always behaved odd around people. They had never been loved. Never learned the trick. We had so many things in common. They needed to be around normal people and I needed to be around odd dogs. That's why I needed them infinitely more than they needed me.

"I really need to get going!" I said. "Really, really, really, really."
I was making a complete fool of myself and I felt the wave of the familiar sadness approaching, threatening to knock me down this time, and maybe I would start crying on top of it all. But at that very time, for some obscure reason, my overactive, overcompensating mind decided to bestow on me the occasional random act of kindness, and informed me that Mayona Ness looked disappointed, so I added:
"But I am sure the dogs; I mean *me*, I mean *I*, will love your book! Because I …*they* love you too … your shoes, I mean, too!  Me too... Buckets of universa or - seas, I mean. Need me. To buy shoes...too...soon."

*

Outside the building Josie had to take a smoke.
I also needed to inhale something strong, -large amounts of oxygen was my drug of choice-, and like a dying marathon runner, I stood there with my hands clutching my bent knees, hiding my tears from Josie, behind a curtain of hair, I took a hundred very deep breaths.

"You really need to hang out with people more, Wyn." Said Josie. "You are starting to act really weird."

The door opened and Mayona Ness stepped outside. She gave us both a great smile and said:

"Hello again funny ladies! Want some more autographs? For the dogs?"

Then she laughed for a few seconds at her own joke. Josie said:

"She really needs to get home and read your book, Ms. Ness; she hasn't been on a date for two years now..."

"No *shi-* ... no kidding?" said Mayona Ness. "What happened then?"

"She got divorced! She's been mourning her ex. ever since."

"Well, not exactly *mourning...*" I said.

"Well not exactly laughing your head off, either!" said Josie.

Mayona Ness frowned in a not so very feminine way and said:

"Ok. Tell you what, Wen; join me for a meal so I won't have to eat alone, and you tell me a little about yourself and I will give you some advice, ok? I love a challenge. I also hate to eat alone..."

"I can't possibly intrude on your time...there must be so many ...eaters...daters... I mean ... mean men...no... Not mean men, but men, I mean..."

"Oh, sure! Too many, too many by far! So where do you suggest?"

She whispered behind her hand:

"It's on my publisher! I made him a millionaire. So by all means, pick a good one! Pick the best!"

"The Merlea. Definitely The Merlea." Said Josie dreamily. "But...-"

The Merlea was a very expensive restaurant near the ocean. Three billion Guide Michelin stars as I recalled, and a galaxy away from my world.

"...- it's impossible to get a table there, if you don't make a reservation months in advance."

"Excellent! The Merlea it is, then!" said Mayona Ness.

She smiled at me.

"Can you make it around seven?"

"Yes..." I said. "But- ..."

"When I am through with you I promise you will get a proper date."

"Impossible!"

"Wanna bet? What do you say? Let's continue the discussion over dinner!"

"Come on! You haven't been on a date for two years!" Josie said. "It's about time!"

"See you at seven sharp then!" said Mayona Ness and picked up her cell phone.

Josie and I were staring after her.

"I can't believe this!" I said.

"Promise me to be yourself, loosen up, and have fun!"

"Aren't you coming? "

"Of course not! It's your date!"

"But I don't know what to wear ....what to say...how
to behave...and-..!"
I stopped myself.
"... -*date*? It's not a *date*! Why did you say it is a
*date*?!"
Josie was smiling.
"Just teasing' yah. Keep blushing! Haven't seen you
blush in years and today you don't seem to be able to
stop! So cute!"
She pinched my cheek lightly.
"Josie!"
The look she gave me was filled with tenderness, love
even.
"You know, Dwynwen, there is more to life than ..."
She sighed:
"Never mind. Don't forget the doggy bag."

⁋

When I arrived at The Merlea I was so nervous I could
barely move my legs, because I had to concentrate on
my breathing and my heart rate.
Maybe that's why I couldn't think properly.
Mayona Ness was waiting for me in the lounge
among the ocean blue velvet drapes and chandeliers and
huge bouquets of fresh pink roses, and gave me a broad
smile.
"I'm so glad you could make it, Dwynwen."
She wore her long hair lose, and was dressed in a very
simple lime green linen dress and a soft black

leatherjacket with a matching pair of soft black biker boots. I had changed my black t-shirt with the animal shelter logo into a black t-shirt and combed my hair and even put on some mascara. I figured I wouldn't need any rouge.

We entered the restaurant together, assisted by an extremely polite Maître d'. I was pleased to notice that for once Josie had been wrong; there were no restrictions against wearing old sneakers and torn jeans, as Josie said it said under the four stars on Merlea's homepage. The extremely polite Maître d'. just looked at me for a second, smiled, and then smiled extremely politely at Mayona Ness.

We were seated in a corner next to an open fireplace by the extremely polite Maître d'.

From where we were sitting we could observe the other guests without being observed ourselves. The restaurant was overlooking the ocean and parts of the steep mountain it was built on, and the view made me feel like a bird for a moment. (The odd one with vertigo.) Luckily the sound of the waves outside the huge panorama windows and the cracking sound from the fire in the open fireplace obscured the sound of my violently pounding heart.

"I like this place. It is simple. Genuine. Feels like home." said Mayona Ness and blew a kiss to the ocean.

*"Simple? It's the most extravagant place I've ever been to! We have nothing in common. I thought. What am I doing here? Help!"*

"I can't tell you how deeply honored we are to have you and your friend here as our guests tonight, Ms. Ness." said the extremely polite Maître d'.

"I bet!" said Mayona Ness.

"Caviar will be fine, so let's try the Russian beluga and Absolute Vodka and blini, for starters, shall we?" she said in the next breath.

I might have looked a bit confused because she added:

"You can have three desserts if you want, Wen, if you want to skip the main course, but you must try the caviar. I insist!"

"Please, I'll have what you are having… "

She ordered the house specialty for main course for us both, and when the extremely polite Maître d'. had disappeared she leaned over the table.

"So tell me, Wen, how come you aren't dating?"

"Divorced."

"No reason not to date. I wrote a book about dating. It made me very rich. Dating can be such a wonderful thing you know, Dwynwen. Such a fulfilling thing. In so many ways."

She was so honest I couldn't help but smiling and I told her what I had never told a living soul.

"Ok, because I am gay and not out." I said.

*"There you are."* I thought. *"Maybe I can leave now, throw myself in the ocean on my way out, to make the*

*pain cease, because nobody will ever love me, and what's the point of anything, anyway, and the dogs will find good homes without me, -who am I kidding? Seriously, what kind of a role model am I to any dog, anyway? - and you can remove that smile from your wonderful face that I will never kiss."*

But the smile didn't leave her face. So I continued:

"I know I am a coward and these days there are no excuses. Only that Josie and Kurt, -that's her husband-, are my only family, my only lifeline to sanity, sort of, and he makes horrible jokes and comments all the time about…about…Well, I just don't fit in, anywhere, in any group, and I need ..."

She gave me a warm smile and said:

"It's ok. Same here. Only in my case it is money, and not a Josie and Kurt-thing. "

She laughed gently:

"You can close your mouth now, Dwynwen."

My head was spinning. This was almost too much information for me to absorb. She continued:

"We all need to fit in for different reasons. I was dating Jim Roibus at the time my book was published and he was in the TV-series *"Serenades for the Mighty"*. When my book was released he got a role in *"BAD"*, the cult sitcom and my book started to sell like crazy. In episode twenty three you can actually spot my book for couple of minutes… He is gay, too, by the way."

"I could never have told…" I said. "Not in a million years…"

"I guess I have gaydar and you don't. But I bet you can spot a sad dog in a million miles!" she said.

We stopped our conversation for a little while when the tray with the caviar server and Vodka and blini arrived.

"I have this knack for publicity I guess." She continued, nodding appreciatively to the extremely polite Maître d'.

"According to Feng Shui money is pure energy and well, let's say I am very fond of ... energy. *Skål*, Wyn!"

We toasted and tasted and the taste was beyond my wildest expectations.

"I guess... In my case, in my world, I can only tell if someone likes me because they lick me." I said.

"Oh gosh, I would love that!"

*"To lick me!?"* I thought and felt myself blushing.

"To live in your world, I mean."

The smile spread from her mouth to her eyes and to avoid her eyes I took another sip of the ice cold Vodka.

She was silent, but I felt her eyes on me.

"...so I could lick you." She added after a little while.

She was observing the effect her words had on me. She wasn't smiling.

Her voice was touching me, playing me like an instrument, making the words and their meaning and their melody reverberate in the deepest hidden places of my being, those delicious words from her mouth spinning invisible liquid fiery threads between our bodies, penetrating my very being, so intimate, so promising, and my imagination could feel her tongue watching me and her eyes licking me, an her mind tasting my fears and delight and my head was spinning, pounding, hungrily ....

The only thing I managed to say was: "*Oh.*"

Mayona Ness was real, and she was sitting so close to me, watching me being assaulted by my hidden sexual fantasies and images and longings; eating Russian Caviar and watching me; and I knew she knew what I was thinking, what I was feeling; and I knew she wanted me, as much as I wanted her, but I had no clue why, because I simply wasn't the type anyone desired and she was the type everyone desired.

*"Is this a date? A real date?"* I thought. *"I don't know how to cope with the real thing!"*

"Are you like this with the men too?" I said, my voice almost inaudible.

"No. That's research."

"What am I?"

"Pleasure I hope?"

I didn't know to interpret her words. Maybe I was wrong, but for a nano-second I thought I detected a spark of fear in her eyes. Perhaps she was a little less self-confident than she had had me believe.

"You could tell about me?" I asked, secretly wondering what had happened to my voice.

"Yep."

"In a room filled with people. Why me? Because I was the only one laughing at your jokes? All of them I mean, even the ones that weren't supposed to be jokes?"

"Well, I usually try not to laugh too loud at my own jokes; after all I have heard them all before. But I must confess I am so damned funny it hard sometimes!"
She smiled but all of a sudden she looked very serious. As if she was confiding in me.

"I'm not joking. You know, sometimes I am so damned serious it is funny!"

"You have no idea. No idea…"
She took another spoonful of Beluga, closed her eyes and moaned:

"How hard it is…."

"…to be or not to be gay Mayona Ness."
Then she looked at me and broke out laughing. When the tension left me, I started to laugh so hard I turned my glass of over, and like a genie in the bottle the extremely polite Maître d'. appeared at our table smiling and immediately refilled my glass and bowed gently and disappeared in thin air. I asked:

"So how could you tell? About me?"

"I'll give you all the directions you need over at my place."
I didn't have the courage to ask her what she meant by her comment. But my entire body was overcome by the most exquisite blend of fear and desire.

*"What next? I have absolutely no experience?"*

Perhaps she could guess what went through my mind, because she said:

"Don't worry; I am very, very good at what I do. And trust me; I have exquisite taste in women."

"You do? But why me, then? I don't get it...?"

"You will."

"I will?"

"Get it."

"It?"

"I have mirrors at my place, everywhere... You will see!"

"Why me, Mayona?"

"Why?"

"Yes, why?! I bet you are surrounded by ... *gaydars.*"

There was a sudden tenderness in her eyes, a sudden softness, and yet, a fire somewhere behind the softness. Just like my body; all softness except for the fire in the centre, where the fire from her eyes spread in my most secret places.

"A hint?"

"Yes please!"

"The headline of the last chapter is "*The truth about love and desire.*"

"It sounds interesting..."

"Yes it is." She said. "I can read it to you. Afterwards."

*ℛ*

Six months later we were relaxing on our huge four poster bed, Zoë and Zigma and Gaia the Zenon on my side of the bed, and Gelt and Ruble and Zloty Dow Jones on Mayona's side, and she was reading to me and the dogs from *"How to expand your heart without a gazillion dollars. Or – how to do the right thing in a life of wrong turns."*

"What will you do for publicity, Mayona?"

"Get married!"

She looked me deeply in the eyes.

"Please! I love you!"

"… And the dogs." She added.

So I smiled and said "Yes."

∿ THE END ∿

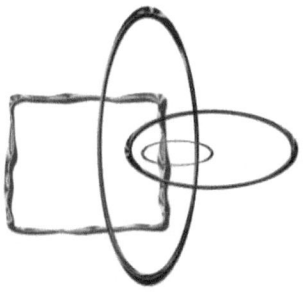

## *"Harmony of the Spheres"*

"Where are you going, Mama?" asked Sophia. "I don't want to stay with granny! Please Mama! Don't go!"

Her little girl's eyes were big and accusing and her lower lip was trembling as she looked up to me and refused to let go of my leg.

"Mama will be back soon and then we will do something really fun, just you and me!"

"Listen, Mum!" I shouted to the woman on the couch. "One last thing before I go; if you let Freddy inside my house again I kick you out! And I mean it!"
She rolled her eyes and made a vulgar sound.

"And please take a shower, will you!" I added.

"A whore and a dyke! That's what *you* are! I feel sorry
for your kid." the woman in the sofa retorted, smiling
triumphantly and her voice was filled with contempt.
Life is supposed to be beautiful, isn't it?
But it wasn't. Not for me.

I had a young daughter to support and a mother who
would have been dead for real, and not just looking it,
many abusive husbands and boyfriends ago, if it hadn't
been for me.
I couldn't afford a baby sitter for either of them.
I didn't use drugs or alcohol like she did, and I didn't
give away sex for free.
I grasped for the real world; the good world of my
childhood dreams through Fiona, and I tried so hard.

Fiona sent a fancy car to pick me up this time. The
chauffeur opened the door for me, as if I was celebrity
material, and when I slipped down into the black leather
backseat I could easily have indulged in a dream but
didn't.
What's the point of dreaming?
We arrived at her big estate through the wrought iron
gates.
   "With regards from Ms. Z." The chauffeur said and
gave me a white card.
Blank?
I smiled.

Carte blanche.

She had her own sense of humor.

Obviously she had forgiven me.

As I stepped out of the car I saw Fiona standing there, on top of the hill, in front of her big house, watching me slowly walk all the way up to her, on shaky legs in my high heel shoes, and even from the distance I could feel she was smiling.

Music was pouring out into the blue summer's night, through the open entrance door behind her, and blended with the hot, sensual summer fragrances.

I could hear loud female voices, and laughter, and in Fiona's wild and friendly garden the birds were having their own party.

My legs felt weak all of the sudden. I felt as if my blue, simple dress and high heel shoes were impregnated with my mother's harsh comments and spiteful glances. Then I remembered Sophia's words: *"You look like a REAL princess, Mama!"* and smiled.

Fiona was breathtaking as usual in her simple black silk pants and suede jacket. She would always be breathtaking. It had nothing to do with genes as you might expect at a first glance. I had often reflected that Fiona's soul might have been born in any physical body and turned it into something exceptional, whatever the odds, just from sheer will power and charisma.

She never let anybody close but was sexier than anyone I had ever met in my life.

She had inherited one fortune and made another one herself, more for the sake of the challenge than because she cared about the money or needed it. Fiona was very generous with money, -it always arrived in my account the day after-; and there was always more of it than I dared to dream of- and still; kind as she always was nobody could be as brutal as her, in her sweet detached ultra-sophisticated way.

Fiona would never be poor in her life; she attracted money and, (because of it) people who were attracted to money.

People like Naomi...

"So you came!" Fiona said in her smoky voice.

"Yes."

"What made you? Finally?"

"You, Fiona."

"I can be quite persuasive, can't I?"

"Quite irresistible!"

"And you are such a rotten liar."

I detected something in her eyes, a shadow of pain, mixed with a sudden flash of anger.

"So; what's' on the agenda tonight?" I asked.

She just smiled.

"Always the impatient one."

"Tell me? A hint! Where tonight?" I asked.

"Amuse me! Have a guess!"

We stood on the top of the marble stairs, in the space between the vast openness of her wild garden and the elegant entrance hall.

I recognized her perfume; Joy, the second most expensive perfume money can buy, and I smiled. Yes, Fiona definitely had her own, very subtle sense of humor.

She touched me lightly on my shoulder.

There was a feeling in her soft blue eyes that I might have interpreted as desire, but decided not to.

Time stood still for a moment as we stood there so close, separated by nothing but the truth.

I might have indulged in a dream for a few seconds, and let the moment sweep me away and rest in a parallel universe of possibilities for a few delicious seconds.

I might have but I didn't.

"How many?" I asked.

"You decide."

"When? Where?"

"You will see."

"Men?"

"No men. I know how you feel about men."

"Thank you."

*"Thank you. Thank you."*

"You are welcome. No big deal. "

She observed me for a while as a wave of relief swept over me, and I laughed when it dawned on me that there might actually be some real pleasure in stall for me that night.

"How is the little one?"

"Fiona..." I pleaded.

"What?"

"Please...don't ... don't talk about ...her... here... now..."

"Why not? I owe her your presence here tonight, don't I?"

She straightened her back, surprised by the flash of anger her voice revealed to us both. Her eyes were impenetrable, hard almost; as if for a second she almost forgot she could buy anyone. Then she smiled again and said:

"Come on! Let's pretend I am the perfect hostess, shall we?"

She took my hand and led me into her house.

The music inside was so loud I could feel it on my skin. I recognized Selene, Stella, Louise, and Moneta dancing, and Mahogany with a drink in her hand, talking to Brianne, and Maryanne and three new girls I hadn't seen before. They were all Fiona's type. She had several types and most of them were represented here tonight.

My heart was beating very hard now, and I realized I was looking for Naomi. When I couldn't see her I was both relieved and struck with pain. I had persuaded myself that I was over her. What's the point of thinking about her?

But my body didn't know that I couldn't love her anymore. My body didn't recognize the superiority of my rational mind and responded the way it always did. I felt a stab in the centre of my being; a stab so acute I couldn't breathe for a second. Perhaps my body would never stop loving her and would forever expose me to this kind of pain whenever I went inside this building, or heard someone mention her name.

I knew I had to be careful and watch out for my sadness; when it leaked out like this; it seemed to paralyze me for a second, make everything go blank except the notion of pain and loss; and I knew Fiona didn't arrange parties just to watch sad people.

The new girls mistook my reaction for jealousy and smiled; their smiles were a mix of feelings; if Fiona found me interesting, it might be worth the effort to get closer to me and find out why.

Only Fiona didn't smile.

"Nice to be back, isn't it?" she said.

I looked around the room. For some reason I always managed to forget how beautiful it was inside these walls, the dark oak floor and sand colored walls where old tapestries hung next to modern art.

Maybe my mind tried to protect me from the pain of the emerging memories but now they returned. Memories of perfection, the kiss, the words, the love, her voice... *Naomi...*

The music was loud and sensual; playing games with my emotions and my body, and slowly but persistently it was turning me on, making me moist in the right place.

I started to move my body to the rhythm of the music, slowly getting in the mood for sex. I enjoy sex. Enjoy it a lot. I haven't always, though, but there were no men around to remind me of old days. Not this time. So, yes, I was definitely getting in the mood, letting the music touch me everywhere. The room had a panoramic view of the big oval pool outside where three girls were skinny dipping, playing and touching each other in between kisses.

"My compliments on the guest list, Fiona...." I said, smiling, nodding.

"The night is long. And so is the guest list." She replied.

"You gave me carte blanche. What did you mean? Anyone? All of them? Where?"

Fiona was silent for a second. Then she said, softly, without any pretence.

"Tonight ...I want you to be with me."

"Oh, I-I- ..."

This was a new script.

She had never wanted to have sex with me, or anyone else for that matter, she just wanted to sip her secret herbal tea, and watch me with others, one, or two, three or more, men, or women, or mixed, observing us, very close, as an intricate piece of art; a living statue with many limbs, but never participating herself.

Whatever confidence I had managed to build up inside for the night, was lost in an instant, and of all things imaginable, of all reactions possible; I felt myself blushing.

My body must have found it fit to compensate for all these wasted years of non-blushing because at this instant I turned crimson.

She smiled and suppressed a laugh behind her beautiful strong hand.

"Look at you! I don't believe it! A bad, bad girl like you! Blushing!"

I wished I hadn't. It gave her even more power over me and reduced my self-respect to an absolute minimum. I should be able to control myself; I needed to be strong now, strong and in control.

I guess the fear and discomfort was written in my face because she said:

"You don't like me a whole lot, do you?"

"I wish it was that simple..." I said.

"It's because of her, isn't it?"

"Maybe."

And I remembered how Naomi had told me that night; *"I am not one of them. I can't be bought. I'm different."*

"Oh, my, oh my; what I wouldn't pay to get to know what's going on inside that head of yours!" Fiona said and stomped her foot impatiently, playfully.

"Money? It's always about money for you, isn't it? All of it?"

I don't know what came over me, or why my sudden lack of self restraint, but, the very moment I had pronounced the words I realized my mistake, and I could hear the accusations in my voice; but too late.

And she turned her back on me in a very elegant turn, almost as if she was dancing a tango.

A small gesture but to me as loud as a slap in the face.

Two of the girls who had been standing close and observing us while they were kissing, noticed the tension between Fiona and me and took the opportunity to approach her, and to have their moment in the spotlight.

She turned her attention to them and immediately made them laugh.

She ignored me completely as if I had dissolved into thin air.

I wouldn't have minded.

Actually I would have welcomed it.

Outside the big windows the sky was dark blue and sprinkled with stars and I reminded myself that when I returned home I must tell Sophia about the stars and endless space.

I must tell her how we are all stardust, parts of the same miracle of life and how the universe is vast and forgiving; so forgiving there is always light somewhere; always a miracle waiting to happen, especially for little miracles of life, miracles like my little Sophia.

I would tell her that the water in our eyes tastes like the water in the sea because it's the same water, and really, I scolded myself; seriously; money is pure energy; creative energy; so who was I to judge Fiona really, when money itself, or rather, my lack of that form of energy, occupied my own thoughts for most of my awake time, and drained me of joy....

There was a soft hand on my shoulder. I drew my breath and prepared myself for her verdict.

"Fiona?" I said my heart beating violently.

But she just smiled.

"We are such stuff as dreams are made on, don't you agree?"

"Definitely, Fiona."

"...and all that jazz?"

"That too-...absolutely ..."

"So let's rock and roll then!"

The nervous knot in my stomach loosened up a little as she took my hand again and led me up the stairs. She opened the door to a small room where there was nothing but a big black four poster bed and purple silk sheets.

Suddenly nervous I said:

"Fiona...I don't know what came over me...I want to ...apol-"

"Hush, baby!"

I looked around the room to get a hint of what she had in mind for the evening but she took my face between her soft hands and forced me to meet her eyes.

"You and me. Nothing kinky. Just you and me tonight. I promise."

She undressed me slowly, like I was a precious gift and she had waited impatiently for this moment.

"I have watched you. I know how you want it!" she said, and kissed me for the first time.

Afterwards she held me tenderly in her arms, my back against her soft breasts, kissing my neck, inhaling the scent of my hair, touching me. My outer world persona, my body, my mind, my soul, all parts merged into one.

The authentic me.
This was a perfect moment and not a dream.

She played with a strand of my long blonde hair. Put it
in front of her mouth, over her lip like a moustache.
   "*Butch? Moi?*"
We laughed for a long, long time at her silly joke. She
sighed and said:
   "You are my drug. I always loved you. More than
anyone."
   "Don't use those lines on me, Fiona, please."
   "Lines…?"
   "Clichés about … love. Please… don't! It's not…
nice. Especially not now!"
   "Now is the perfect time."
   "Now is the cruelest of times."
She bit her lip and turned around.
   "You have serious trust issues!"
"*And you have a very selective memory.*" I thought.
   "Why *her?* Why …*Naomi?*" she asked and the name
made me jerk as if I had received an electric shock.
And Fiona noticed my reaction. Her grip was suddenly
tighter, harder.
   "Why Naomi? Why …her? Of all the girls?" she said.
"I want to know!"
   "Why?"
   "I need to know! One day I will tell you why."
I was silent for a while.

"She told me she loved me. Nobody had done that before."

"Come-on! I don't believe that!"

Fiona dug her teeth into my flesh and I could feel my nipples harden again.

"Neither did she. But she persisted. And finally I believed her..."

"Do you miss her? Ever?" she asked, pretending to sound neutral.

I closed my eyes.

*"Do I miss her? Always?"*

There was a void in me, from everything that had stopped living, an aborted feeling, which led to a sense of freedom of sorts, a black garden of nothing, a void, which I resorted to sometimes and returned from, sleep-walking, stronger, indifferent; a place of nothingness from which I returned to be a mother to my own mother and to my wild and ferociously intelligent child. But a stranger to myself, lost in a black void.

*"Why are you crying, Mama? Please don't cry!"*

"Nothing turns out the way I expect. Ever." I said.

"With me it's the opposite. Things always work out exactly the way I want. Except-..." She interrupted herself.

"Except?"

"Well. You know what they say: "*No rule without exception*"!" she said. "But you avoided my question; do you miss her?

"I trusted her. Finally I trusted life...love... the future...The power of love...and...then...when I finally trusted her...when I finally dared...to trust... to love..."

"Then...?"

"I can't talk about it. Maybe because... I just don't get it; that's all."

She leaned back and released her grip on me.

"The little one was conceived here, wasn't she? The same night you and Naomi-..."

"What difference does it make?" I interrupted, suddenly afraid.

"Tell me! What do you tell her when she asks about her father?"

"Why do you want to know all this?"

"Because... I do. So just tell me."...and she added, softly: "...please!"

"I have told Sophia that his name was Pythagoras and that he was from the Harmony of Outer Space-..."

"I love your mind." She said. "I love you."

I didn't know how to respond, so I didn't; and just continued telling her about that night. I said:

"At the moment of... conception I thought of Pythagoras. So I have told Sophia that her father is out there dancing to the music of the spheres ...always... always in Harmony"

"Did I ever tell you I love the way your mind works!"

"Yes, you just did! Expensive thoughts, though! Now she wants to become an astronaut. So she can visit him and show him her drawings!"
We laughed a little.

"So the little one wants to become an astronaut?"

"Well; that's what she keeps telling me! Three years old, lives in a damp in the middle of nowhere, and has a live-in rude suicidal man eating zombie for a grand-mother, and a- ...a- ... well, me for a mother;..."
I turned away from her glance so she wouldn't notice that my eyes had filled up with tears.

"... can you believe the ambition of that child?"
I started to laugh but Fiona was serious.

"Yes, I can. She is your child and she is the child of Pythagoras, why shouldn't she; she deserves the best. Trust me; she will become an astronaut one day."
I looked at her.

"How can you be so sure?"

"Didn't I just tell you, things always work out the way I expect them to?"

"Somehow I love the way your mind works, too, Fiona! Especially your sense of humor!"

"My house and life and body are solid manifestations of how my mind works!"
She allowed no further comments on the matter but silenced me in a kiss that almost made me faint, despite the fact that I was lying down.

"I like how your body works. When you let me."
I said, and this time I wasn't mortified when I blushed.
It felt okay.

"Please let me! One more time!" I begged.

"You are so innocent, my love." she said. "Look at you; blushing again! Can't resist you when you are blushing like that!"

"Then don't fight it, Fiona!"
And she didn't.
She loved it.

*

Afterwards she kissed me again, very tenderly and for very long and said:

"I would like to meet her."

"You wouldn't like my neighborhood, Fiona!"

"Bring her here. Bring her to me!"

"Are you sure?"
She thought for a second and smiled at me.

"Well, on the other hand; maybe we should all go to Greece?"

*

## Yes.

*

*"Everything changes and nothing perishes."*
*Quote by Pythagoras, mathematician, mystic and scientist*

*580 b.c.*